A Quiet Little Town

A lighthearted science fiction story that could happen to you

Fred E. McMichaels

A Quiet Little Town

A lighthearted science fiction story that could happen to you

Fred E. McMichaels

ISBN 978-1-7326046-0-5

Leanpub

This is a Leanpub book. Leanpub empowers authors and publishers with the Lean Publishing process. Lean Publishing is the act of publishing an in-progress ebook using lightweight tools and many iterations to get reader feedback, pivot until you have the right book and build traction once you do.

Contents

CONTENTS

About the Book

A science fiction story set in the not too distant future about growing up, problem solving and taking risks. Based on actual incidents, cutting edge technologies and medical research with a slight stretch of the imagination. A fast-paced easy to read story, not to be taken too serious. But you might want to slow down and reflect on the issues raised related to where our world may be headed.

Chapter One – Background

Farthington is a small town in upstate New York nestled in the ski country just north of the Pocono mountains and the Pennsylvania border. For many of the town's fifty thousand or so residents the summers are too short, and the winters much too long. Although it is not uncommon for passionate skiers to travel hours to enjoy their favorite winter sport, few of the natives ever venture out to challenge the well-known slopes surrounding the little village. Most Farthingtonians think bears have the right idea in winter. A trip to the Chestnut Hill Mall to examine the latest additions to McFealy's pet store and maybe a stop at the Farthington bookstore is about as much excitement as most local residents can take on a cold winter's evening. So when spring arrives it's never too soon in Farthington.

Summers in the little village bring few warm days, but it was one of those hot and sticky ones in August when Patrick McMichaels sat on the edge of his bed at 116 Cherry Street talking on the phone to Mike North, his life-long best friend from down the street. Despite their bond, recent years had seen the boys' lives move in separate directions. They were sixteen years old and it was the year 2023.

"Hey Pat, are you going to Golden Lake on Saturday?"

"Can't Mike."

"Ruth-Ann's going to be there."

"Schoolwork. My grades are the pits," explained Pat.

Mike North was an accomplished downhill skier. His bedroom walls were filled with Farthington Gazette sports writeups. Through the years, broken legs, lost teeth, bruised ribs, and numerous trips to the Farthington General emergency room had failed to derail the boy's goal of one day reaching the Olympics. Mike had worked diligently with one of the most highly touted ski instructors from the northeast who just happened to be his father. His skill had rapidly matured far beyond what most of the experts had ever imagined. An aggressive skier, Mike had shown personal discipline and dedication carrying his Olympic dream to the brink of reality. If he had a weakness, it was his lack of finesse and style– key ingredients in the critical eye of an Olympic judge. Nevertheless, what Mike lacked in textbook technique was certainly overshadowed by his unrelenting drive and unshakeable belief in himself.

As for the experts, there was still plenty of disagreement. Was little Mike North from Cherry Street really Olympic material? Up to now the thick-skinned youngster had proven the experts all wrong. And nothing, or at least nothing anyone could foresee at that moment in time, was going to stop him.

At sixteen Mike was facing his toughest challenge. Plans were set for the North family to move West where the ski season was longer and the competition stiffer. His coach agreed. Mike needed to get out of the local limelight. The two boys had not spoken of the move, but since the "For Sale" sign appeared in front of the North residence they had been spending more time together. Neither boy doubted it was the right thing to do, but still an unspoken sadness seemed to pervade the old neighborhood these days.

"Mike, meet you out back for a quick game of hoops."

Pat hung up the phone as his father entered the room.

"Pat, how was school today?"

"Ummm... Ok, I guess."

"Just Ok? How's your chemistry project coming?"

Pat glanced toward the ceiling and then back at his father.

"Look dad, by the time I finish college nobody will care about the stuff they're teaching us today."

Mr. McMichaels looked sternly at his son.

"Yes dad, I know what you're thinking. But Mr. Osgood told us everything we're learning today in school will be old and outdated before we get to use it. He says the world is changing too fast for traditional education to keep pace."

Through their early years it was Mike North who had struggled to find direction in his life. But at sixteen it was his best friend Patrick McMichaels who was losing his focus. In the early years it had been Pat the dare-devil and Pat the creative thinker. It was Pat who in the summer of their ninth year decided the two boys needed a secret project. That was the summer of the now infamous McMichaels-to-North tunnel. After watching one of Mr. McMichaels' favorite old-time Steve McQueen movies about a prison escape, Pat had come up with the idea. A tunnel. Yes indeed. They would build a tunnel between their homes. And they would build it alone. Afterall, it made perfect sense. It would simplify things on rainy days.

Today Fred and Janet McMichaels look back upon the incident with a smile. But at the time they found nothing humorous fully expecting to be paying off lawsuits well into Fred's retirement years. The tunnel actually turned out to be an amazing architectural achievement defying for days a number of longstanding civil engineering principles– not to mention Newton's law of gravity. Eventually, however, physics won out and few from Cherry Street will ever forget the day six fire trucks pulled up in front of the poor sighted Mrs. Murphy's home. They were looking for the old woman who had called 911 reporting an earthquake in her backyard. It's a wonder no one was seriously hurt, except for Mrs. Resinski's cat Rosie who had gotten loose again that morning. Rosie was almost buried alive. She survived, but hasn't left home since.

But now, at sixteen, it was a more cautious Pat. The boy was changing and he was struggling with the direction of his life.

"Pat, sit down."

Oh no, thought the boy. He glanced toward the door. Fred McMichaels believed learning was best accomplished through real life situations and he was constantly on the lookout for opportunities to apply his theory. But his kids didn't see it that way. They called it "the Fred time-warp." Dad's stories-with-a-lesson simply defied the principle that time moves forward.

"Dad, could we skip the lecture tonight?"

The boy was sitting on the edge of his bed with his eyes avoiding those of his father. He had dreamed of one day working alongside his father out at the lab, or at least that's what Fred thought he was dreaming about.

Pat's father Fred was an engineer at the Jefferson Research Lab in Brintwood. Brintwood was a small town just east of Farthington. But Jefferson accepted only the top students which wasn't exactly Pat's current ranking. The boy was a bright kid, but at this point in his life schoolwork just wasn't high on his list of important things to do.

At sixteen Patrick McMichaels was more interested in a weekend at Golden Lake with Ruth Ann Barber. Fred just nodded and started walking toward the door when Pat suddenly blurted out,

"Dad, do you think I'll ever be any good at anything? Sometimes I feel like I'm living in the wrong place or time."

The words jolted Fred- "wrong place or time."

He instantly stopped in his tracks and turned back toward his son, hesitating for a moment to collect his thoughts before replying.

"I know what you're feeling. Trust me, you're living in exactly the right place and time."

Fred looked at the boy slumped over the edge of his bed.

"But dad, sometimes I feel like my life isn't real. Like it's just a dream."

The boy hesitated, looking down from the edge of his bed. Fred shook his head.

"Your life is real. It isn't just a dream. But if you're not careful life can pass you by like a dream."

"But dad, you know I seem to keep screwing up everything I do these days."

Fred looked at his son, rubbing his chin.

"I need to tell you something that will be difficult for you to understand."

Fred hesitated.

"You don't need to worry about screwing things up. In fact, you can make as many mistakes as you need to and it really doesn't matter."

"Dad, don't you care about my life? You should be yelling at me and telling me to straighten up like other parents do."

But Pat knew his father wasn't like other parents and said things nothing like what other parents say to their kids, like what he said next.

"Pat, if what I told you scares you then what I am going to tell you next will scare you even more. When I tell you your life is real and isn't just a dream that doesn't mean that dreams aren't part of your life and aren't real. You can think of your life as just a practice run. A chance to try life out before you go for real. And you can practice as much as you need until you're ready to go for real."

Fred hesitated, then looked directly into his son's eyes.

"And when you're ready to go for real, you'll know it."

Fred hesitated again.

"There's a master plan, and you have a critical part."

The boy looked up at his father. He was used to his father saying strange things like what he just told him.

Then his father added,

"And remember, you have the tools."

His father turned and headed back downstairs. Pat fell back on his bed. His eyes scanned the slow-moving ceiling fan. Then he looked around his room– football pads, basketballs, baseball bats, soccer cletes, and a single picture of an old-time baseball legend. His father's words echoed through his head.

Tools? What tools? Pat wondered.

Mom sold the electric saw the day after I chased Rosie with it. In the distance, his mother's voice was heard.

"Pat, Mike's here."

Chapter Two – Their own world

It was supposed to be a quick game to eleven. Winners outs. Mike grabbed a rebound, dribbled a couple of times, then let fly with a jump-shot.

"Coach Henson's wife went to a four-day seminar on nutrition," said Mike.

"So what?" replied Pat.

"She said the rules have changed."

"What rules?" asked Pat.

"The rules to figure out what's good for you. If it tastes good, she says you have to spit it out now."

Mike continued to ramble as Pat's mind drifted. He was thinking about what his father had said. Mike grabbed another rebound, and drove to the left side flinging up a wild hook-shot. Pat jumped for the rebound as Mike's elbow collided with his right rib.

"Ugh!" yelped Pat. The ball stopped in front of the garage door.

"What's this?" asked Mike.

"It's dad's. He's working with some advanced virtual reality ideas. Mom says he's trying to prove some crazy idea he has that will help kids when they grow up."

"What's he trying to prove?"

"Don't ask me, but he's been trying to prove it for a long time. It's got something to do with creating a world where kids can learn by making mistakes, even big ones, and no one gets hurt or even yelled at."

"I thought the government made virtual reality illegal?"

"If you don't know what you're doing, then it is. Dad says it can be dangerous. That's why they outlawed it. But my fathers got a license. He's a professional and the kind of virtual reality he is working on Mom says is nothing like what's been done in the past."

Pat reached down and picked up the basketball.

"I probably shouldn't tell you this, but I think they're using VR out at the lab."

Pat muffled his voice.

"They're using it on a secret project."

"What makes you think so?" whispered Mike.

"Well, dad's been pretty tight-lipped, but Lindsey heard him mumbling in his sleep."

"Mumbling what?"

"She said he was mumbling something about finding a way to connect a virtual world to the real world we live in where you could try crazy new ideas without worrying about negative effects. She said he mumbled something about a breakthrough."

Mike looked confused. Pat continued.

"Lindsey doesn't think it's important. But I think she's wrong."

Pat lowered his voice again.

"I heard dad talking on the phone about the same idea to someone at work. He said he got the idea from an old Twilight Zone episode where what people thought was normal was completely upside down from the way we think. Dad says the way to help kids become creative is to get them to think about and be open to ideas that most of us are not comfortable with."

"What kind of ideas?" asked Mike.

"It doesn't matter. Dad says what matters is to get people excited about living and being creative does exactly that. He also told me that if people aren't excited by what they're doing, they should do something else."

Mike shook his head.

"That just sounds like a lot of the same stuff my father has been telling me for years. That's why my dad quit his desk job and became a ski instructor. He loves to ski and he told me if he only had one life that was what he was going to do, even if he didn't make as much money."

"No, Mike. There's more to it. First, you gotta swear you'll never breath a word."

"Ok. Ok. I swear. Now spill."

Mike followed Pat to the back of the garage.

"Virtual reality makes you think you're in another world. They've been using it for training for a long time. But dad says the problem is that these virtual worlds are fake worlds and don't present the real tough challenges that kids are going to have to face when they go out into the real world. So, dad is working on a way to connect a virtual world to the real world. He calls it a hybrid-virtual-real world where kids can learn in a safe way and it's not just pretend.
"

"Where did your father get this crazy idea?"

"Dad said he got the idea from work-study programs they have in college. With work-study programs you learn partly in the classroom, but you get to apply what you learn in a real world situation. I don't understand it, but dad has found a way to teach kids in a safe way, but do it in a real world situation. And what dad is doing goes further by allowing you to play what he calls what-if games."

"What's a what-if game?" asked Mike.

"Did you every wonder what your life would be like if certain things about you were different, or if you just made a few different decisions?"

"Like what things?"

"Like, if you were taller, or smarter, or lived during a different time, or if you were the same as you are, but you just made a few different decisions in your life?"

"Sure. Doesn't everybody wonder about those things?"

"Well, that is what dad calls what-if games. But out at the lab they are taking this idea much further by actually making some of it real by allowing you to test out those other what-ifs to see what happens. Then you can make better decisions on how you live your real life when the time comes to live that one."

"This is really starting to sound like science fiction."

"No. Its real. Close your eyes."

Mike closed his eyes.

"I mean tight."

Mike squeezed his eyelids.

"Now think about what it would be like if you won the Olympic downhill gold medal."

Mike squeezed his eyelids tighter.

"What do you see?"

"I can't see anything. You told me to close my eyes."

Mike opened his eyes.

"How did your father figure this all out?"

"I don't know exactly, but from what I overheard him saying on the phone, I think he found a gate."

Mike opened his eyes wider.

"I'll bet he did, and yur ol man got loose," quipped Mike.

"I can't tell you anymore and you have to promise not tell anyone else. It's a top secret project at the lab."

The Jefferson Research Lab occupied the former site of Klink Industries. Klink was a defense plant before the turn of the century. Jefferson employed two-thousand engineers working in the education field, or so the public was led to believe.

President Wilburn Bradson, a former professional basketball star for the New York Knickerbockers, had won the tight election in the year 2020 based largely on his campaign promise to improve the country's educational system and bring back honesty to government. Both had been in a rapid decline for a number of years. The American people were investing again in the country's youth and Jefferson was reaping the profits. But with only one year left in Bradson's first term, the public was becoming restless.

Where were all the promised results? Where were those better test scores for our kids? And where was that improved quality of life for all Americans?

In reality progress had been painfully slow because the team at the Jefferson lab had gotten sidetracked from their original mission due to some incredible discoveries that could truly revolutionize the learning process. But this would take far longer than everyone thought and the opposition party was positioning itself for a strong run at ousting the incumbent Bradson.

Questions were already being leaked to the media. Questions that could prove embarrassing due to the over-run cost and schedule and the requirements creep of the program. Questions like what was really going on out in Brintwood on the edge of town?

"Look at these wires hooked up to this old astronaut suit."

"Don't fool with it. That's not an astronaut suit. That's part of my dad's latest project."

"Try one on! It's wild!" responded Mike.

"Take that suit off! My dad would go crazy if he knew what you were doing."

"Aw c'mon! You never used to be afraid of your old man. Where's the Pat I used to know?"

It was a good question. Pat had been wondering it himself. Where was the Pat Mike used to know? It was starting to bother him.

"Ok, but only for a minute. Then it will be time to go in for dinner."

Pat put the suit on, and when he did he felt something. But it wasn't exactly a feeling. It was something else. Something hard to explain and it was coming from a long time ago stirring something deep inside him.

Thoughts of the McMichaels-to-North tunnel raced through his mind. The old tunnel. Pat hadn't thought of it in years. In fact, he had tried desperately to forget it. After all, who'd want to remember being grounded for six months. And who'd want to remember all those chores for Mrs. Murphy without getting paid one red cent. And who'd want to remember all those walks with Mrs. Resinski's mean old cat Rosie. But, at that moment, standing in the old garage where he and Mike had spent so much of their lives, he couldn't stop those thoughts from racing through his head.

"This feels really weird. Kind of like 'Scotty beam me up!'"

"I think my dad tried to tell me about this."

"What did he tell you?"

"Dad says if you really want to learn something new you have to be willing to give up many things you've been taught and look at the world in a whole new way."

The sound of screeching tires and the slam of a car door were heard.

"Lindsey's home."

Pat's older sister Lindsey drove a green Corolla Luxury Edition, Toyota's most reliable and best-selling car. It was a gift from her father and mother on the girl's nineteenth birthday. Lindsey was a freckle-faced brunette and a sophmore at Farthington University. She was taking a double major in Cybernetics and Psychology.

On this day her usual cheeriness was missing. She stormed into the house.

"Mom, if the phone rings, I'm not here!"

"Dinner won't be ready for an hour, dear. Why don't you go out back with your brother and Mike. I'll call you when it's time to eat."

But Lindsey ignored her mother and headed up to her room.

When she was younger Lindsey had often played basketball with the neighborhood boys. She had shown a devotion to the game from an early age frequently practicing late into the evenings. Mrs. McMichaels had put up a spot light in the summer of 2016 when Lindsey was twelve. The girl often lost all track of time out back late at night working on her game.

"Fred, why don't you go up and talk to your daughter. She's in one of her states."

This season Lindsey was playing for Farthington University– a strong team with a proven reputation. In her freshman year Farthington had won the state championship as Lindsey had watched from the end of the bench. Three starters from last year's squad had graduated and this year Lindsey stood an excellent chance of securing one of the starting forward roles.

Only a few years earlier the thought of Lindsey as a college forward would have seemed crazy. The girl had always been a terrific ball handler with a natural feel for the game. She had played point guard throughout her high school years. But in the summer between her junior and senior high years– in just three short months– Lindsey grew an incredible eight inches.

Watching her grow out of control caused her mother to panic. She told her husband Fred she thought something must be dreadfully wrong with the girl. There had been no family history of incredible growth especially in such a short period of time.

So, Fred told his wife that he would take his daughter to a specialist to have her checked out. Then he told his wife that the specialist told him nothing was wrong with the girl. He told her that because he didn't want her to worry. He said the doctors told him she was just a normal healthy growing girl, but, in fact, he never took his daughter to any specialist because Fred already knew the truth.

Throughout her senior high school year the top division one college scouts throughout the country aggressively pursued her. Despite this attention Lindsey chose Farthington University. Farthington was her favorite team ever since that cold and snowy night back in the winter of '2014 when she first attended a college game with her family.

But on this day things had not gone well. There were great expectations for this year's team and Lindsey was feeling the pressure. Being a leader on a high school team was one thing. But this was college ball and in only her second year she was being looked to for team leadership. She had stormed out of practice earlier that day angry with the team's poor performance.

"Hi Linz." She growled, then shook her head and rolled her eyes.

"It's awful, dad," she sighed.

"Linz. Remember last year?"

"Sure. We won it all."

"I mean earlier– the shaky start?" prodded her father. She wrinkled her nose.

"Time, Linz. Just give it time."

The girl looked up at her father. She took a deep breath. Then she let it out with another sigh. Mr. McMichaels placed his hand gently on the girl's shoulder.

"You need to have goals, but.."

She interrupted him.

"I know dad. You've told me before. I shouldn't let my goals get in the way of my life. But the first game is only a week away. And they'll be expecting us to be good!"

With Linz, it had always been a battle. They'd been down this road before. Through the years Fred had learned to live with it. And even enjoy it– a bit. Oh sure, he'd gotten frustrated too, at times. But there was something about her– something about that look in his little girl's eyes. There were other times too. Hard times. Times he wondered, hadn't he said it all before? A hundred times at least. And did it matter? Did any of it really matter?

Nineteen years ago Fred and his wife Janet had made a choice. They chose for Janet to stay home with the kids giving up a promising career. And Fred would not pursue an opportunity that might have brought them a larger home, a more expensive car, and maybe even a place by the ocean. Fred's opportunity would have meant changes. Changes he and Janet didn't feel were the right ones at the time. There were dreams too. Dreams of what life would become down the road– a successful business for Janet and Fred pursuing his secret dream.

But now the year was 2023. Fred was fifty-three years old. There were no homes by the ocean. There were no successful businesses for Janet. And time was running out. Fred and Janet had made their choices. And every now and then Fred found himself just wondering what his life would have been like if he had made just a few different decisions.

"What are you two up to?" blurted Lindsey. She had always liked sneaking up on her brother and Mike.

"Linz, grab a suit. This is wild. Checkout the status page with the snake," said Mike. In the year 2023 the snake had replaced the

well-known mouse as the most popular computer-human interface
device.

"Get out of those crazy suits right now!" she demanded.

"Let's shoot some hoops."

"C'mon, Linz. It's just like CyberLand."

"I don't have time," retorted Lindsey. She picked up the ball and
headed for the court. Slowly her brother turned and looked at her.

"Linz, don't you ever feel like playing anymore?"

She stopped.

"What do you mean? I play all the time."

"I don't mean basketball. I mean like we used to."

She turned and stared at her brother. She had felt it. Many times.
Oh sure, it was neat being a college sophomore and driving her own
car. And she loved having the things you're supposed to want when
you're nineteen and everything's going your way. But every now
and then she wanted something else too. She wanted something
you're not supposed to want when you're nineteen. She thought of
the park. Then she thought of her family.

"Ok, but afterwards we must go in for dinner."

She put the suit on and double-clicked the snake.

"We have three choices," said Lindsey as she examined the status
page.

"Decision-Making, Nuclear Physics, or Nutrition."

"Just pick one."

She double-clicked Decision-Making. A message appeared on the
screen. It said, "Check Safety Belts." They sat down in front of the
computer and fastened their belts. She double-clicked again.

Fred McMichaels was standing in his dining room. Fred was a
driven man– not by wealth or power. Just driven. And on this

hot and sticky August day he couldn't get his mind off his latest software creation. Is it possible? he wondered. Could it really work? He rubbed his chin. That morning Fred had gotten up early to make a minor modification to his latest software program. The idea had come to him in a dream. He had gone out to the garage where he compiled and downloaded the change. He hadn't yet found the time to test it. After dinner, he thought, I'll head out to the garage and give her a test run.

Mrs. McMichaels opened the back door and yelled to the kids. There was no response. Where are those kids? she wondered. She called again. But still there was no response.

"Fred, those kids are out there in their own world again. Would you please go out and tell them it's time for dinner."

Fred walked out the backdoor into his yard. His eyes passed the basketball court and then slowly panned the open garage door. He noticed a basketball lying on the ground. There were no kids in sight. From a distance he noticed his computer screen. A message was blinking at him. That's strange, he thought. He moved closer. Then he read the message. Instantly his face paled. He fell back tripping over an old pair of cross-country skis laying on the garage floor. The flashing message read: "MISSION IN PROGRESS."

He mumbled to himself as he fumbled at the keyboard selecting the status page. The page read, "Number of Active Players - Three."

He read the words. Then he read them again: "Number of Active Players - Three."

The words made no sense to him. He turned toward his newly installed role player station. He noticed that the seat belts were fastened and the ON light was lit.

"That's funny," he said to himself, "I'm sure I left those belts unfastened this morning."

His eyes moved to the garage wall where he had left four role player suits. Only one remained. The picture was becoming clear to Fred–

painfully clear. Fred's minor software modification was apparently functioning quite nicely.

"Janet!" yelled Fred.

Mrs. McMichaels ran to the garage.

"What is it, dear?"

She looked around. There was no response and she saw no one there. Where had they gone? she wondered. Was this another one of Fred's games? she thought to herself. She peered downward. Lying flat on his back was Fred. His eyes were fixated on the garage roof. "Fred! Fred!" she screamed.

Her husband continued lying perfectly still saying nothing at all. But he did manage to slowly raise his index finger on his left hand and point it directly at the blinking message on the computer screen. Janet turned. She read the message. Then she calmly turned back to her motionless husband.

"Fred, dear, we knew this day was coming. It shouldn't be a surprise. I've heard other parents talking. No matter how much you prepare they say it's still a shock when they finally go."

Fred's eyes were closed, as if by keeping them closed and believing hard enough he could somehow make it all different.

Chapter Three – A secret

"Where are we?"

It startled Pat to hear his sister's voice. Mike pointed at the long and winding broken brick steps just a few feet in front of them.

"I wonder where they go?" questioned Pat. Mike shrugged.

"There's only one way to find out."

Mike started to climb and Pat and Lindsey followed. It was a damp and chilly evening. With each step Pat could feel the thick clumps of un-mowed grass between the broken bricks beneath his feet. It was getting dark and the fog was rolling in. In the distance a faint shadow of an old house appeared. Pat turned and looked back. He could no longer see the path below and it made him feel uneasy.

"Mike, uuh... I...I'm not so sure we should be going up here."

Mike glared at his friend. Then he turned and kept moving forward until he reached the front door where he raised his right hand and knocked softly twice. Pat and Lindsey stayed back a safe distance.

"I don't think anybody lives here," said Pat as he turned and started moving away.

"Not so fast," replied Mike.

The boy wrapped again on the large wooden door, this time with greater conviction. But still there was no response so they turned to go.

Then, suddenly, Mike stopped as he raised his right index finger to his lip.

"Shhh."

A faint shuffling sound was heard coming from inside. Pat turned and looked directly at the large front door as slowly it creaked open, and as it did an urge came over him– an urge to turn and run as fast as he could and never look back.

It wasn't the first time he had that feeling and whenever it came it reminded him of something he wanted desperately to forget.

Pat McMichaels had a secret and he had kept it close for a very long time. He never told anyone about it and he thought he never could.

"Can I help you?" said an elderly gentleman. He was standing in the doorway.

"Well, you see sir, it's like this. We were out in our garage on Cherry Street in Farthington, New York and my stupid brother somehow got us lost in our own backyard."

Pat looked at the man as his sister tried to explain. The man's long grey beard couldn't hide his eyes. There was something about the man that plainly scared the boy.

"We've been expecting you."

Expecting us? thought Pat. Why would he be expecting us? We weren't planning on getting lost. They followed the man into the house and down a long and narrow hallway leading to a dimly lit room. The man flicked on a small lamp.

"It's a shame," the man continued. Then his voice trailed off as he peered out the only window in the room. He seemed distracted. Pat was having trouble concentrating too. Random thoughts kept flashing through the boy's mind. He'd lived with it for such a long time that it almost felt like it was now a part of him. He never talked about it to anyone because he thought if he ever did start talking he probably would never be able to stop.

"Pardon me, sir. What's a shame?"

His sister's voice jarred the boy back from his lost thoughts.

"It's a shame so few take the time to think it through."

The old man rubbed his chin, and slowly turned his head away, then he quickly looked back.

"But you are different!"

Lindsey glanced at the boys puzzled by the old man's comment.

"If you could just give us directions to Cherry Street, sir, we would be off and on our way?"

"Not so fast. Not so fast. First, let me show you around the place. I've lived here a long time and I rarely have visitors."

The man's words stirred more memories Pat wanted to forget. He was twelve at the time. His friends had told him about a different old man. They said he lived with rats and was crazy. Everyone in the neighborhood seemed to believe it. He had to be crazy to live like that. Pat recalled that night. He could feel his heart pounding then and it was pounding again now like it always did whenever he thought of it.

Of course, it was over now. He knew that. But he knew it never could be completely over. Time froze that night, at least inside the boy. He recalled the feeling lying under his bed– so still, so motionless, so all alone as he waited, believing it was just a matter of time before everyone would know the truth about what he did and they would come and take him away.

Chapter Four – A private world

"This is where my uncle Joe and I used to clean our fish."

The old man carried on with his stories. Stories about his uncle Joe and going fishing with his old dog Blue as they moved from room to room. The stories grew more and more disconnected as the old man became more and more confused unaware he was repeating himself, seeming at times to just slip away. But through it all he never stopped watching Pat in a chilling sort of way.

Mike began to laugh.

"He's nuts. The crazy old man doesn't know what he's talking about."

Mike's words angered Lindsey as she scolded him, and told him to stop. She was thinking about a Sunday years ago when her family visited one of her mother's old and dear friends who lived in a nursing home. Patrick came along, but was too young to understand.

She recalled thinking at the time how good it was that people lived so long, but not that way. The people in the home told disconnected stories too. She had never met the woman in the bed next to her mother's friend, but that Sunday there was no one else to listen to her. The woman called Lindsey Julie and rambled on like the old man and every few minutes she'd ask Lindsey if she would take her home.

The old man also reminded Lindsey of the way her brother often acted when he was younger. The boy was so easily distracted. She had enjoyed taking advantage of him whenever she could get away with it.

She recalled the large department store where her parents often shopped and her brother would crawl between the racks of clothes losing himself in his own private world.

When he would hide, she would hide too just to see the fear in his eyes when he would start to think he had been left there alone.

She had always been convinced there was something wrong with her brother. He never seemed to learn. Only a week would pass, and he'd do it again– lose himself again in his own private make-believe world. Why isn't he more careful? she often wondered.

That Sunday in the nursing home she thought about what it would be like to grow old. The old woman had gotten overly excited thinking Lindsey was someone she knew who had come to visit her. And then the nurse came and gave her something the nurse said would make the woman feel better. But Lindsey knew it was something to make her feel nothing at all.

"Let me show you around the old place," the old man was repeating himself again.

"I've lived here such a long time."

Then he turned and asked,

"Could I help you?" as if his guests had just arrived.

"Yes sir, I think you could help us. Could you tell us the way to Cherry Street? We'd like to get home for dinner."

He raised his arm and pointed toward the window.

"Do you see those roads?"

Lindsey squinted, but the fog was too thick to see anything as she peered out the window.

"Some have sharp and dangerous curves."

Then he paused and looked directly at Pat.

"Do you know what happens to the ones who don't take the time to think it through and make good decisions?"

"No sir."

"They don't make it." He shook his head grimly looking downward.

"Oh come on!" retorted Mike.

"You're just trying to scare us. We know this is just a game."

The old man slowly turned. Then looked straight into Mike's eyes with the most piercing stare the boy had ever felt. The entire room chilled.

"You think this is just a game?"

Then he quickly turned and looked at Pat.

"And you! Look at me boy! You think it's fun to hurt people?"

"No, sir." The man hesitated as he rubbed his chin.

"If you're looking for just a little fun, then you've come to the wrong place. If you want to play little boy, then you can head right back down those steps and just keep running. Any road will do."

Lindsey looked at her brother. What she didn't know, and what nobody else knew was that Pat McMichaels wanted to turn and run and keep running—just like the old man said– until he was as far away as he could get, and never ever look back.

But where would he go now? Which road would he take? He had tried to escape the feeling before, but wherever he went that feeling went with him.

"If you're staying," said the old man, "then you all better sit down."

He pointed to three chairs pushed against the far wall. They all slowly walked to the chairs and each took a seat. No words were spoken for what seemed to be a very long time. But it had now become clear to our three young lost travelers that they wouldn't be home for dinner tonight.

Chapter Five – Never dream again

Janet McMichaels wasn't a dreamer like her husband Fred. But she did look forward to the times when she could slip away and on this day she was slipping away with her latest Anne McCaffrey novel as her husband Fred paced.

"They'll do fine, dear." She looked up at her husband just as the doorbell rang.

"Hi Fred. Is Mike here?" Fred was staring at his shoes. It was Roger North, Mike's father.

"Hello Roger."

"What's with Fred?"

"He's just wrapped up in his work again," explained Janet.

"Judy had another bad week at the office. We're thinking about getting away for a few days. Is Mike here?"

"Fred sent the kids on a little mission, Rog. Why don't you and Judy take a little time for yourselves. Mike can stay with us for the weekend."

"I wouldn't want Michael to think he was missing anything."

"I wouldn't worry about Mike missing anything Roger." Fred glared at his wife. Roger nodded, as Janet shut the door. She then turned and squeezed her husband's arm.

"Just give it a little time, dear."

Fred was feeling nauseous. He couldn't stop thinking about what he had done. He had designed that software all alone. It wasn't something he was used to doing. At work he usually operated as a member of a team, sharing responsibilities and bouncing ideas off his teammates before making crucial decisions.

But this crazy idea had come to him and no one from work wanted any part of it. Even Fred knew how crazy it was. But a part of him actually believed it could work. Fred also knew all the things that could go wrong. But things going wrong weren't new to Fred and that never bothered him before. But this time was different. This time it was about his kids.

When Fred awoke that morning he was so excited that he just forgot to think. Oh why! he was thinking now, didn't I take the time to think it through! Now he'd have to live with his decision for the rest of his life.

He glanced at the picture of his children on the marble top table. He shook his head. Fred McMichaels had a dream and it was a dream he had for a very long time. But now he was wishing he would never dream again.

Chapter Six – It's your decision

They were led into a special room that reminded Pat of his grandmother's church with its high ceiling and etched windows. Each window seemed to tell its own story. Pat recalled the few times he had been in the church with his grandmother. He had never been able to figure out exactly what the stories on those windows were trying to tell him. There were other things in the room that reminded him of his grandmother too. The Victorian chairs and the mahogany table. His father hated mahogany. On the table lay blank paper, pens, disks, a computer and a number of very old and worn hardcovered books.

The boy's eyes reached the far edge of the table. He was suddenly startled to see an English looking man standing there. At first, he didn't recognize the man, but after a closer look Pat realized it was the same man who had met them at the front door and given them the tour of the house.

The man was acting different now. His speech was polished and his mind appeared alert. The man was smiling as he walked around the far side of the table toward Mike.

"Please make yourself comfortable." He motioned toward the Victorian chairs.

"Have you been to Virlingreal before?"

Mike looked at Lindsey. Then he turned back toward the man shrugging.

"We are pleased that you have come to help us."

He smiled again. Pat kept looking at the etched windows, and the furniture wondering why his father hated mahogany.

"As we told you before, we are lost, and it couldn't have happened at a worse time."

"Why is that young lady?"

"We need to get home to Farthington," answered Pat quickly. "You see, my good friend Michael is going to the Olympics. And he is running out of time. And my sister plays basketball for Farthington University. They're the defending champions."

The man looked at the boy. Then he stroked his beard.

"And you, son? Where are you going in such a hurry?"

"Well, that's just it," replied Pat.

"I need to get home to figure that out."

The man shook his head.

"Well then I cannot be of much help to you. I've never heard of this Cherry Street, nor any place called Farthington. Are you certain it's in New York State?"

"Yes. I'm certain of that. It's been in New York as long as I've lived there."

"And just how long is that?"

"All my life."

The man shook his head again.

"Of course, it's your decision," the man continued looking at the boy.

"But sometimes the best way to figure out where you should be headed is to help someone else along the way."

"I don't know how we could help," said Lindsey.

"We know nothing about this place you call Virlingreal."

"Oh, it's not so different from wherever you come from, although some people do seem to think differently around here. And where there are differences you can always learn, if you keep an open mind."

He pointed to the bookshelves along the far wall.

"We have plenty of material. Of course, you won't have time to read it all. But you can learn as much as you need to get started and then you can learn more as you go."

The man hesitated, looking at Pat again as he picked up a book from the table and started thumbing through it. Then he closed the book and set it back down on the table. He seemed to be waiting to see how the kids would respond.

"Can't you get someone else to help?" asked Lindsey.

"We can always get someone else. There are always others who are willing to learn, but for you there is no better time than the present."

Lindsey glanced at the boys and then turned back looking directly at the man.

"Just what is it you want us to do?"

"I wish I could give you more details. And I suppose it isn't necessary to retain all of you."

He looked at Lindsey.

"I know it's not fair to ask you to stay. You have your own life. If you did stay you might miss a game or two."

He turned and looked at Mike.

"And we could never expect you to stay with the Olympics so close. But you! "

He was looking at Pat now.

"Even if the others decide to go, you must stay."

Pat turned and looked at his sister. His eyes were bulging out of his head. Then he looked back at the man.

"You mean– alone?" The man didn't answer.

"Sir?" Pat tried to get the man to say more.

"You don't need to keep calling me sir. My name is Hank."

"Ok, Hank, I can handle this. But there are just a few details I need to know," replied Pat pretending to be more confident than he actually was.

"Details?" questioned Hank.

"Yes," replied Pat.

"Like how do you pause this game in case I get tired and need to take a break?"

The man scratched his head.

"Look, you don't seem to understand. There are games you play for fun and there are other games—serious games– that have nothing to do with the kind of fun you're talking about. Do you understand the difference?"

He was staring directly at the boy and Pat was starting to feel the sweat beading up on his forehead. The boy's pretense of confidence was rapidly fading and his old memories were starting to flood back like they always seemed to do at the worst possible time.

Maybe I could get to a phone, thought Pat. There must be a phone somewhere around here. But what then? Who would I call? What would I tell them? I couldn't possibly tell them everything, he thought to himself. It frightened him just to think of all he had been through. He was now sixteen with his whole life in front of him, or at least that is what he thought. And he thought he had finally put that nightmare of a night four years ago behind him.

There must be another way he was thinking now. Surely a reasonable person would understand. We were just playing. That's what kids do. Just playing. But would the police understand that now? He looked at his sister and then his best friend Mike. She would have been driving her teammates hard at practice now and he would be making his final preparations for the Olympic qualifiers.

I need to let them go, and handle this myself, he thought. I'll just play along until I can figure out how to get home.

Chapter Seven – A big mistake

It was late one evening back in 2011 when Fred first got his latest crazy idea. He had just returned from his regular monthly visit to his chiropractor, Jay, and their usual stimulating conversation had got him thinking. He looked out the back window of his home watching his daughter playing one-on-one basketball with her brother. She was just seven years old at the time, but he could see the potential even then. The girl had a natural feel for the game and he hadn't even given her any serious coaching tips yet.

She was quick, could dribble as well as anyone, could shoot the eyes out of the ball, and her defense was incredible, as she stuck to her opponent, in this case her brother, like glue often stealing the ball before he realized what was happening. And most important she had the desire. She was already dreaming at seven years old of being a college all-star and even one day playing pro ball.

But Fred knew the one thing that was almost certain to keep the girl's dream from coming true. No females in his family, or Janet's family, had ever grown to be more than five feet five inches tall. Fred knew he could help the girl build strength and endurance through an aggressive exercise program. He knew there was no limit to how much she could improve her shooting and dribbling and defense through practice. But what can you do about your height?

Height was pretty much determined by your heredity and the DNA your parents passed down to you, or at least that was what most people thought before the twenty-first century.

But out at the Jefferson Lab, as part of Fred's secret project they were aggressively applying the results of recent DNA human genome studies to help kids learn faster, better, and improve the quality of their lives. Although it was still in the early stages, scientists were already proving they could affect physical characteristics, including height. But so far the studies were limited to monkeys.

Soon, thought Fred, they will be doing this with humans, and isn't it a shame that we may be just a few years away and his daughter would miss this great opportunity. That is, unless Fred could get his daughter into an early study program.

He knew the technology was a long way away from FDA approval, but that never stopped Fred before. He had, in fact, participated in an early study of a new procedure to solve his Atrial Fibrilation, known as AFIB for short, before the new procedure was FDA approved and the results turned out fine.

He had talked about his idea with a few colleagues out at the lab, but they told him it was still too soon to try the latest procedure with humans. But that didn't stop Fred from doing a little research on his own and when he did he discovered a new technology that just might make his daughter's dream come true. It was called CRISPR technology. CRISPR stands for Clustered Regularly Interspaced Short Palindromic Repeats.

In 2013 scientists in Boston at the Broad Institute developed a method to use CRISPR to edit the genome in human cells, but the ethics of when CRISPR should be used was still being hotly debated. This was largely because the possibilities were endless including the potential to edit embryos to eliminate many hereditary diseases, as well as editing the DNA sequences that affected physical characteristics such as one's height.

By 2023 CRISPR was commonly being used to cure a number of previously incurable diseases, but it had been made illegal to be used in a performance enhancement way such as making people stronger, smarter, or taller.

The rationale was clear as this kind of "playing god," as many in the news media referred to it, would likely lead to professional sports teams growing their athletes through selective breeding. Many argued the technology would lead to a world where being a great athlete would become less a matter of hard work, and more a matter of just having enough money to breed the "perfect" athlete.

But Fred wasn't thinking about all that in 2011 when he just couldn't get his little girl's dream out of his head. The crazy idea kept festering inside him, and two years later in 2013, late one night he went on Amazon.com and ordered a vile of CRISPR in liquid form.

Unfortunately, since Fred had become so obsessed with making his daughter's dream come true, he just didn't take the time to step back and consider all the possible ramifications of what he was doing. He just started giving the CRISPR a little at a time to his daughter, mixing it in with her morning breakfast a small dose at a time so she wouldn't taste it. It was six years later when she was fifteen that the drug started taking effect, and that is when his wife Janet started getting concerned.

And it wasn't just her height that was affected. There were other changes that family members and friends started noticing in the girl. She had always been a bit obstinate when it came to her opinion on certain matters, but at least she used to listen to alternative suggestions and give them due consideration. Lately, however, a number of close friends started noticing changes in her personality and her focus. And these were not just positive changes.

She had previously been a reasonably balanced girl. Interested in not just sports, but other things as well, such as music. But now at fifteen years old, as she started to grow out of control, her focus on just basketball seemed to be overwhelming her, and her friends noticed whenever they tried to mention it to her she had a very short fuse and would often burst out with uncontrollable anger. And she was spending more and more time at the gym, and as a result her school work was degrading.

That is when Fred started wondering something else. Had he

adequately thought about all the possible consequences related to what he had done to his daughter? And that is when Fred also started wondering if maybe he had made one of the biggest mistakes of his life.

Chapter Eight – Dreams that count

The old man placed the large platter of scrambled eggs in the middle of the kitchen table. He whistled as he scurried about.

"Sit down and eat hearty."

He had risen early to prepare the morning meal. Lindsey and Mike had decided not to leave Pat alone. They figured he stood a better chance if they hung around to help him. The girl had stayed up past two-thirty the night before reading about Virlingreal.

She learned about a deadly disease called Goat Mountain Spotted Fever. It was known as the V-bug. It was officially reported to be caused by the bite of a rare tick, but people in the know in Virlingreal knew that wasn't the real cause.

Lindsey from all that she had read the night before had reached the conclusion that this V-bug was an important part of the mission the kids had found themselves on. She couldn't put her finger on exactly why it was important, but she just had a feeling about it.

"Sir, we need to learn more about the bug."

Her eyes moved from the eggs to the man. He was fumbling with his knife trying to butter the toast. He set the knife down alongside the butter dish. He wiped his hands on the soiled apron tied loosely around his waist. Then he looked up.

"What do you know of it?" he asked peering at the girl curiously over the top of his glasses.

"Just what I've read here."

He squinted, and leaned forward to get a better look at the book the girl held in her hand.

"You shouldn't be reading that."

He reached to take it from her, but before he could she snapped it back glaring at him. The man took a step back. The girl's obstinance had caught him off guard.

"It is about the bug, isn't it?"

"No, you've got it wrong." Then he looked away.

Slowly the girl stood pushing back her chair and gazing down at the book which she had set on the top of the table. The night before she had seen pictures of sick children who had contracted the V-bug. She glanced at her brother. She had decided not to tell him what she had learned knowing how he felt about small bugs, especially ones that made buzzing sounds.

She was now thinking back to that afternoon in August years earlier. It had been raining non-stop for days. It was her father's idea to take a hike on the trail behind Farthington University. But this time was the first time they heard the buzzing sound. Her father was bitten first, but he wasn't allergic like her brother. It was the look on the boy's face she remembered most. He told her later it was the first time in his life he thought he was going to die.

Lindsey kept watching it swell all the way home. She knew what her brother wanted. He just wanted to get home. At home mom would know what to do. But when they got home, Pat's mother wasn't there and the boy had to trust his sister. Lindsey told him it would be ok, but not because she believed it. She told him because she knew it was what her mother would have said.

"I'd like more jam and toast," said Pat.

No one was listening to him. He reached across the table dipping his knife into the open jar. Then he spread the jelly evenly across his toast. Lindsey was tapping her foot rhythmically on the floor. It was a habit she often exhibited when her patience was running thin. It was just one of many of her habits that irritated her brother. She cleared her throat.

"Look, I've already missed one practice and I'd really like to help you but–"

Lindsey hesitated in the middle of her sentence. The man was looking out the window again appearing to ignore the girl.

"Sir?" she said. "Are you listening to me?"

The man didn't respond.

"Sir! Please listen to me! I haven't got time for your games!"

The girl had become known for these sudden outbursts and they seemed to be getting worse as she aged, especially when she felt under pressure. She seemed to startle the man as he turned and stared at her.

"Games? We've talked about games before and I don't think you kids seem to get the difference between serious games and games kids play. What do you know about games, young lady?"

"Plenty. I've been playing basketball all my life and I am very serious about the game of basketball," she snapped back at him.

The man chuckled.

"Well, why don't you tell me what you know?"

"Ok. I will. First, I know the difference between games that count and games that don't count. I know basketball counts. And I know whatever game you're playing doesn't count," she replied snottily.

"And why doesn't my game count, young lady?"

"Because your game isn't real. This whole place isn't real. It's nothing but a dream."

"And dreams don't count?"

"Your dream doesn't count because it's not a real dream."

The man jerked his head back, as he pointed at Mike at the same time.

"And what about his dream? Doesn't his dream count?"

She looked at her brother's best friend. His face was pale.

"If he makes it, it counts."

"And if he breaks a leg, or just isn't good enough? What if he finishes second, or third, or fourth? Does it count then?"

Mike's face turned stone-white. Lindsey's forehead was heating up and she felt like her head was about to burst from the anger she held inside her. But just then Mike unexpectedly broke the tension.

"It's true that I have a dream. But I know the difference between my dream, and my life. I am going after my dream with every ounce of strength inside me, but my dream won't get in the way of my life."

Mike's response caught Lindsey off guard. She didn't know what Mike was talking about. She had never thought of the possibility of not making it in basketball. And she had never thought of anything in life being more important than her dream. She stared back at Mike.

Then she turned and looked straight at the old man. She didn't know exactly what this game was about, or even if it was a game. But she was now convinced of one thing for sure.

All this business about bugs, sickness, goals, and dreams was all somehow connected. She didn't know how, but she just had a feeling it was all connected and she also now believed that finding themselves in this strange land was no accident.

She looked at Mike and Pat.

"Finish your breakfast boys. We've got everything we need from this old guy."

Then she turned and pointed out the window.

"We need to head down that road right now and figure out what the heck is going on in this strange land and what we need to do to get back to our lives in Farthington."

Chapter Nine – A backup plan

Fred and Janet had always been interested in education. When their kids were young they had to make a choice on schools. While Farthington had been a great place to raise a family, the neighborhood where they lived had changed over the years.

When Fred did his graduate studies at Farthington University he worked with a Professor McHenry, who believed in the Texas method of education. He told Fred that his education up until then had amounted to feeding his brain from books and it was now time to stop memorizing facts and turn his brain around to become more creative.

Professor McHenry explained to Fred that he had given a math problem to a student who did not know the problem he was given had never been solved, and the results led to the student's PHD thesis and recognition of a major breakthrough in the field of mathematics.

"If you believe the problem you are working on is impossible to solve, you have no chance of solving it," Professor McHenry explained. He went on to say,

"Creative young minds can do amazing things if we don't get in their way with our own limited thinking."

Fred and Janet chose to send their children, Patrick and Lindsey, to the Jackson City school district, a small suburb of Farthington, where they used Mastery learning which has similarities to the Texas method.

From his educational background Fred knew that mistakes were a normal part of learning. After modifying his daughter Lindsey's

DNA using CRISPR, Fred realized his mistake. While kids need guidance, Fred now also realized that too many parents—including himself– go overboard trying to force a child's future direction.

Simply put, trying to mold a child into a parent's hope for that child can often lead to unintended consequences and far worse results than just leaving the child alone to figure out their own future.

As Fred was coming to grips with his mistake, he learned something else about DNA referred to as methylation.

Methylation is a process that can change the effect of a DNA sequence without changing the DNA sequence itself.

Methylation factors include environment, exercise, what you eat, and just plain old hard work. Recent Methylation research was proving that these factors can have a much more powerful influence on a person's physical and mental abilities than what had previously been believed by most modern researchers and physicians.

This led Fred to start thinking about what would have happened to his unmodified daughter, if he had just left her DNA alone. Who is to say, Fred now thought, that Lindsey wouldn't have become a great basketball player even if she was short?

In fact, throughout history there had been some great NBA basketball stars who were under six feet tall including Muggsy Bogues at five foot three inches, Calvin Murphy at five foot nine inches, and Spud Webb at five foot six inches. And if you have great speed and shooting skills who needs to be a great rebounder anyway?

But now Fred was wondering what he could do to fix his mistake. He was constantly trying to impress upon his children the importance of taking risks and not being afraid to make a mistake.

He would tell his kids,

"there is no such thing as failure. You always get results. And remember, you can always make another decision."

He had learned this way to think from a book he read "Unlimited Power," by Tony Robbins, and he kept those words on his office door as a constant reminder.

In the case of his daughter, Fred knew when he was applying the CRISPR idea that it might not be the best idea in the world. And so he made another decision, just in case.

When Lindsey was five years old Fred saved one of her baby teeth when it fell out thinking he could use it to extract her DNA if needed in the future. He got this idea from his massage therapist, Mary. He then had the tooth frozen to preserve the DNA.

When Fred started to give Lindsey the CRISPR when she was nine years old, he also had her cloned using her original DNA from the baby tooth. He had, of course, not told Janet about this backup plan. When Lindsey's clone was born, using a surrogate mother, he gave her up for adoption to a couple across town. The girl was named Erin and she was now ten years old.

Now that Lindsey, Patrick, and Mike were off on their mission, and with Fred believing now he might have made a big mistake, he decided it was time to come clean with Janet.

So, Fred first explained to Janet how he had bought the CRISPR from Amazon and put it into Lindsey's breakfast, a little at a time, so she would not taste it.

As crazy as this story sounds, Janet just sat quietly listening and looking at Fred. This is because she had lived with Fred for more than half of her life and she knew that somehow she had managed to survive all his other crazy ideas. Finally she spoke.

"Fred, I am trying my best to stay calm. I am telling myself this is not really happening, but it isn't working. You have done some insane things in your life, but this one takes the prize as the craziest thing you have ever done!"

Fred nodded, agreeing with his wife, as she continued.

"So, Fred. You are telling me you modified our daughter's DNA probably seriously affecting her future life, and now you think you made a mistake. Do I have that right?"

"Basically, dear. But give me a chance. I haven't told you everything yet. You see, I thought ahead about the potential consequences of my decision. I thought the whole thing through, just in case things didn't go according to my plan."

Fred had a big grin on his face now, as if he thought his wife would somehow be proud of him for thinking ahead. Janet wasn't smiling.

"Fred, please continue. But why do I feel I don't want to hear what else you did?"

"Well dear. I created a backup plan. You know how I always like to have a backup plan."

Janet had closed her eyes and was shaking her head back and forth.

"I don't know if I want to hear about your backup plan, but please tell me quickly before I explode!"

"Actually dear, just in case this taller version of our daughter didn't work out so well I took some of Lindsey's original DNA which I smartly saved from one of her baby teeth when she was just a child."

He hesitated, smiling again, as if she would be doubly proud of him for coming up with this backup plan, and then he continued.

"And I had her cloned using a surrogate mother. The girl's name is Erin. She is a great kid and she lives just a few blocks away. She is being brought up by my good friend JR Trip, who works with me out at the lab, and his wife Sue. I was thinking of asking my good friends Bob and Carol to raise her, but they live too far away just outside Boston.

I also got her a part-time job out at the Jefferson lab where I have been keeping an eye on her as she has been growing up."

Janet was staring back at Fred with an expression that can't be adequately captured in any known words.

Fred continued.

"You are going to love to learn, dear, that Erin is a musical prodigy. She graduated from high school at nine years old and is the youngest student ever accepted at the Boston Conservatory!"

After continuing to just stare back at Fred with that same indescribable expression for what seemed like eternity, but was probably only about two and one-half minutes, Janet slowly began shaking her head back and forth as her mouth opened with the following word slowly coming forth.

"I take back what I said about modifying Lindsey's DNA being the craziest thing you have ever done. Cloning her and giving the clone to neighbors a few blocks away beats that hands down!!"

Then she raised both her hands placing each on the sides of her head as if she were trying to keep her head from exploding.

"So, Fred. You are telling me my real daughter is being raised a few blocks away, and I am bringing up some mutant version of our daughter. Do I have that right?"

"Janet, you have to understand Lindsey is our daughter. Parents often have some great kids and some others that don't turn out exactly as they hoped for. We just have to accept our kids as they are."

"I just have one more question?" asked Janet.

"What is that dear?"

"Please tell me you haven't modified or cloned anyone else."

"Of course not, dear. I was thinking of using CRISPR on Mike to give him a better shot at the Olympics, but I decided to wait and see how Lindsey turned out."

Chapter Ten – A drug

Our three lost travelers hurriedly finished their breakfast and headed down the first road they came to in the direction the old man was pointing the evening before. They soon came upon another little old man working diligently by the side of the road.

"Sir, could you give us a little help?"

Lindsey tried to get his attention, but he stayed focused on his job. The man wore heavy tarnished gloves as he busily went about trimming the grass. His eyes were hidden by the perspiration stains on his wire-rimmed glasses, and his skin was brown and leathery, probably from too much time in the sun.

"We are here because of the bug."

He continued to pay no attention to the girl, until finally he stopped to take a deep breath. He looked up, but said nothing. He seemed to be sizing up the three strangers who had come upon him. Then he cleared his throat and turned pointing toward the dense forest about thirty yards from the edge of the road.

Lindsey squinted through the bright sunlight shining directly in her eyes coming from the direction the old man was pointing. As she reached up shading her eyes with her left hand a voice that sounded like that of a child was heard coming from beyond the trees. The voice was too distant for her to make out the words. She began moving toward it plodding through thickets of tall grassy weeds.

She turned making sure her brother and Mike were following, but was surprised to see the little old guy tagging along. He had removed his gloves and cleaned his glasses making it easier for her to see his face.

"Ouch!"

She had accidentally stepped into a pricker bush. She reached down carefully taking hold of a branch moving it away from her foot, then carefully pulling her leg out. She shook her head and smiled recalling a story her mother had told her when she was young.

She had only a vague memory of the incident, but she did recall being in her crib and hearing the loud noise. Her father was out of bed in a flash. He was still half asleep and didn't take the time to get dressed, or to think about what he was doing. He just chased the noise out the door and into the dark in the backyard of their home on Cherry Street.

Janet said it looked like an explosion and it lit up the whole sky. She said she watched from the second floor porch near Lindsey's crib as she heard Fred cry out.

"He had run into my rosebush," she said, "and I couldn't stop laughing as I listened to him screaming at my rosebush in the dark in just his underwear."

They reached a clearing where a river came into view. She counted fifteen pitched tents just a few feet from the river's edge and a number of young children busily moved about. A blond-haired boy who looked to be no more than ten was cleaning fish and an older girl was tending to a fire near the tents.

Another older and taller lanky boy with stringy blond hair who looked to be about thirteen or fourteen was fishing down by the river. He was using vine and a stripped tree branch for his pole.

As they moved closer Lindsey noticed that the boy who was fishing had a nasty rash just above his right ankle. Further down the river a round-faced chubby boy was scrubbing clothes, and a curly-red haired girl was hanging the clean ones to dry. All the children wore similar clothing made from animal skins and none of the children wore shoes. Behind the red-haired girl high up on a hill on the other side of the river in the distance could be seen a graveyard.

Lindsey glanced at her wristwatch. The thought that she would have been at practice if she were home, crossed her mind. Just then a scream was heard. The lanky boy had collapsed. Two of the older children rushed to help him and were carrying him to a nearby tent.

As they passed Lindsey noticed his rash appeared to be infected. She turned toward the little old man.

"Can we help?"

He shook his head.

"It always gets worse in the heat. There isn't much we can do once they go bad."

Pat looked up.

"What do you mean?"

The man gazed out over the river. Then he raised his hand and pointed.

"It's called Snake River. They say its banks are a breeding ground for poisonous mosquitos, and deadly ticks. But that's just what they say."

The man took two steps back, then stopped and started shaking his head. Then he looked down.

"That boy was one of the leaders. He was warned by his parents, but he had this crazy idea and he wouldn't give it up."

"What crazy idea?" asked Pat.

"It doesn't matter. What matters is that what he did was a big mistake. And to make matters worse, then the stories of what he did grew. And more kids came because they wanted to learn more about his crazy idea. More bad kids who didn't listen."

"I thought they were sick?" blurted out Pat.

"They were sick," replied the man. "Seriously sick."

"Why do you keep calling them bad?" The man looked at the boy.

"It was wrong for those kids to do what they did. They'd been warned."

"But you said they wanted to learn."

"That's right. But they were trying to figure it out on their own and that just led them to make mistakes."

"But isn't it normal for kids to make mistakes when they're learning? You have to let them try things on their own. Otherwise they'll never learn to solve problems using their brain. That's what my father keeps telling me."

The old man just shook his head and snickered at the boy.

"We tried that allowing mistakes stuff, but all hell broke loose. When you let them make mistakes it's dangerous. And it takes a lot longer for them to learn that way. So, the guys on the top decided everything would work better if we just told the kids what to do, and not waste time trying to get them to figure it out on their own. And ever since everything happens in a nice orderly fashion around here."

The ill boy had returned to the edge of the river. He reached down to pick up his makeshift fishing pole. He staggered. The right side of his body shook. Lindsey rushed over to help steady him. He jerked his arm away. His jaw was clenched tight.

"I don't need your help!" he snapped rudely at her.

I just thought–" He quickly interrupted her.

"I know exactly what you thought. You thought as long as you were here you might as well give a bad kid a little help."

"Look, I didn't choose this!" she snapped.

"And you think we did!" he snapped back.

"All I wanted–" He interrupted her again.

"I know exactly what you wanted. You wanted to make yourself feel better." He turned and started to hobble away, but the girl wouldn't let it go.

"If you are sick, why won't you let us help you."

The ill boy stopped and turned back looking directly at Lindsey.

"We aren't sick. In fact, we are the only ones in Virlingreal that are even close to being healthy. They didn't like the fact that we had different ideas. We just wanted to make a few changes in how things are done around here. They called our ideas crazy, but they weren't crazy at all. Our ideas were just different, and they didn't want to change. Most of the kids in Virlingreal have been given a drug to make them act like the guys in charge want them to act."

"What kind of a drug?" asked the girl.

It's called CRISPR. Have you heard of it?"

"No. What's CRISPR?"

"It's a drug that can modify your DNA and can affect a person's physical or mental characteristics. They figured out the DNA pattern that causes kids to think on their own. They used the drug to modify that DNA sequence so all the kids just follow orders. There are just a few of us who refused to take the drug so they called us sick and forced us to live here in these tents near the river. They said we were bad because we had our own ideas. Any kids who have their own thoughts that don't conform to the ideas of the big guys on top are called bad kids, and they say we have this made up disease they call the V-bug. But it's just a made up story to scare everyone into following their orders without thinking on their own."

"Is there a way to reverse the effects of the drug?" asked Lindsey.

"Sure, you can program CRISPR to do lots of different things as long as you know the DNA sequence of what you want to change, and the DNA sequence of what you want to replace it with. In fact, I noticed you are quite tall. I'll bet they could use CRISPR to make you shorter if you think you would like that."

Chapter Eleven – Someone else's life

The little bespectacled man glanced back at the straggling boy as they headed back from the river to the road where the man had been working.

"What are you waiting for son?"

It was a good question. Pat had been waiting a lot these days. And now he was thinking– just thinking about something his father once said to him about not letting life pass him by. Could life really pass him by, he wondered– like a bus passes by?

And– if it could– where would he be then? Would he be caught in someone else's life? Was it possibly to actually live someone else's life? He thought of the crazy old man and the rats. He wondered if the crazy old man was living someone else's life. Who would ever choose to live the only life they had that way?

But maybe it wasn't his only life, thought Pat. Maybe he just made a little mistake along the way and maybe it wasn't his real life. Maybe it was just a practice life for the old guy just like his father had told him. Maybe he just wasn't ready yet to live his real life.

Pat looked up. The others were out of sight, and the thought of being left alone scared him. So, he started to run, and then he ran faster until he caught up.

"Are they still going bad?"

Pat was looking at the little man. He was back to feverishly trimming away acting like he hadn't even heard the boy's words.

"I want to know!" he demanded in a harsh tone. The man's head jerked up.

"We're having fewer casualties these days. Only the Controllers think now. They're the workers who make sure the orders from the guys up top are carried out," he replied in a matter of fact tone.

Pat squinted.

"The rest of us just do what we're told. We're called Components. That's what makes everything work so well here in Virlingreal."

The man's words triggered thoughts inside Pat's head. It seemed like someone was always telling him what to do or yelling at him.

"Keep alert, Pat!" his baseball coach would yell. "Do what you're told. Don't forget to use your brain, Pat!"

He had always thought he was using it. Just differently. But deep inside he felt something wasn't right when all he was doing was following someone else's orders. Being alive meant being free to the boy. Sometimes he needed, in the worst way, to just let his mind go to think whatever crazy thoughts entered his brain just as his father had told him.

But now he was thinking again of that night—and whenever his mind went there something would get in his way. They were just investigating. Looking for a little proof. Trying to learn something. We didn't think anyone would get hurt.

He recalled sitting at the supper table that evening listening to the usual dinner chatter. Nothing seemed different, but it was. It was all different, but only Pat knew how different everything had become. Dad talked about work and mom talked about their upcoming vacation– a vacation Pat would probably miss. He recalled looking at his sister and thinking how much they had argued through the years. He couldn't remember why. For an instant he thought he might miss her, but probably not.

Pat wasn't stupid. He knew the score. The police in Farthington were good. It was just a matter of time. He said it again in his head. Just a matter of time. And the next day it was all in the newspaper. "Jay Wilson," it said. It was the first time he had seen the man's name in print. He read it again, this time he said it aloud. "Jay Wilson." The article made him sound like somebody real– like somebody who mattered.

"Bad" was the word they used to describe the boys, and it stuck in Pat's brain. Maybe it was the heat, he thought. It was a hot night. He knew he had done some bad things in his life. But he had never thought of himself as bad. Bad kids were born that way, or at least that's what he always thought. It was just a matter of time.

"Aren't the kids allowed to think at all?" He just wanted to know and so he blurted it out.

"When you let kids think, the next thing you know they start to dream and that's where all the trouble starts," replied the little man.

Pat liked to dream. He had been dreaming for the longest time of one day building his own software game. He had talked to his sister about the details. She had written a software game in her Cybernetics 152 course at the University. Pat had decided that in his game– at least at the beginning– the players wouldn't be told very much about the game. He thought it would turn out better that way. He wasn't even going to let them know that it was a game.

"I'm just going to let them think it's real," he had told his sister. He got the idea from something his father had told him. She didn't like that idea. She didn't think it would be fair. But this was going to be Pat's game and anyone who wanted to play Pat's game would have to play by Pat's rules.

"In my game everyone will learn as they go and it will be ok to make mistakes."

His sister just shook her head pretending not to listen.

"And they will learn what they believe is really important. Not what someone else thinks is important."

She ignored that too. He looked up at the little man again. He was still working at a feverish pace.

"If the children have dreams, sir, why don't they go back to school so they can learn how to make their dreams come true?"

The man squinted out of the side of his eye.

"They tried that letting everyone learn idea too. It really fouled things up even more than letting them think."

He squinted again.

"You're not from around these parts, are you, boy?"

"Pay no attention to my brother," quipped Lindsey. "We're still working out a few of his bugs."

"Not surprising! Back in the uncontrolled thinking days it was plenty worse! Today if anyone's caught thinking on the job–" He stopped cold right in the middle of his sentence.

"Had a friend who got caught thinking on the job. The next day he was back in the shop." The man looked down shaking his head.

"I saw him a week later. I almost didn't recognize him. They used the same parts. But it wasn't him." He drew a slow breath. Then he looked away toward the woods.

"But don't you be thinking there aren't still fighters around these parts. There's still plenty of underground thinking just like those kids near the river."

His eyes sparkled as he said it.

"But be careful who you talk to. Some get real touchy when it comes to–" He stopped and pointed to his head.

Pat glanced at Mike. He thought he knew him almost as well as himself. Mike was a fighter. Pat often didn't see his friend for long periods of time, especially during ski season. But Mike always called when he needed to. And then they would talk. The two boys talked about most everything and when they had a problem they would think it through together. They had talked the night before in the old house up on the hill.

Pat recalled the look on his friend's face as he stared at the book. It was laying on its side covered with dust. Pat reach for it, but Mike's hand got there first. He picked it up, and brushed the dust off. Pat listened as his friend read. Intelligent robots. They had been secretly built– fifty of them. Advanced Learning Research Components or ALRCs for short.

The book said they looked real, but they were just machines. Machines that acted smarter than typical software components. They used a new innovative approach to model the way people think. But that's where they got in trouble because their actions proved erratic. You couldn't predict what the robots might do, just like real people. A threat to the national security they called them. And so the billion dollar secret project was cancelled and the ALRCs were scheduled to be dismantled in November of 2003.

Pat rubbed his chin. Huum, 2003. Before I was born, he thought to himself. He recalled when he was very young and his sister would plead with their father.

"Tell us a story about the olden days, father," she would say.

"It was 2003 and back then people worried a lot less," Fred would respond. Then he would drift off into some made-up tale that would grow and grow. Father just had a way of making up whoppers of tales. And everyone would smile. Dad would glance at mother. We'd glance too. She'd act like she wasn't listening. She'd be reading one of her Anne McCaffrey books or playing Sudoko. Acting like she wasn't listening or didn't care what Fred was saying. But the moment would always come when she'd roll her eyes and come out of her chair with the same words always rolling off her tongue,

"I can't take this anymore!"

Out of the room she'd fly and father would always smile.

Mike was still reading. Pat glanced toward the floor. A few inches from his left foot a soft-covered green book had fallen open.

Stuffed between two pages was an article from a back issue of the Virlingreal Gazette. It was dated, 4 January, 2004. Pat couldn't take his eyes off the title of the article. It read, "Three ALRCs missing!"

The article stated that a government audit had found three of the ALRCs scheduled to be dismantled had not only turned up missing, but one was believed to be infected with the V-bug. The device, when last seen, was reported to have a rash on its wrist and a lesion just above its right ankle.

Pat eyes locked on the final sentence. It stated that the missing ALRCs had been the responsibility of the project leader, a Frederick E. McMichaels.

After reading this article the night before, Pat closed the book and sat back in his chair. His eyes panned the far side of the room. ALRCs? Fred McMichaels? Was it just a crazy coincidence? No. This was no coincidence. Pat knew everything was connected. And now he knew for sure that his father was in the middle of it.

"Sir, can you tell us where we might learn more about the underground thinking?" asked Pat.

"Head for the edge of town. Look for a small grey shack on Swampy Pond Road. Ask for Aerial. Now be off with you! I must get back to my work."

Chapter Twelve – A space vessel

The old shack looked on the verge of collapse. The lawn hadn't been mowed for months. Pat carefully examined the stamp-sized front porch where books and magazines were strewn most of them face down. The porch boards groaned with each step.

"Keep an eye out for spiders," said Lindsey as she swiped a cobweb from her hair.

Pat stopped suddenly, startled by a noise coming from inside. He lurched back knocking Mike off the porch splashing into the mud. Two eyes peered out between the red faded curtains covering the only window in the front of the tiny grey shack.

"Sorry Mike."

Pat reached down giving his friend a hand. Mike gave it a yank pulling Pat off the porch into the mud with him. A scruffy unshaven old man in long red underwear and boots suddenly appeared on the front porch staring at the boys. Pat couldn't take his eyes off the barrel of the man's shotgun.

"If you kids want to go swimming there's a better place down the road a piece."

"Sorry sir," said Lindsey. "We've come a long way and are very tired. We're looking for Aerial."

"State your business."

"We're from Farthington, New York and a few days ago we were out in our garage on Cherry Street. We were just playing, minding our own business and then something strange happened and we haven't been able to find our way home since. We were given your name as someone who might help us."

The man squinted at the girl suspiciously. Then he turned glancing quickly at the boys.

"First, let's get the mud-swimmers into dry clothing. Then we'll fill your bellies with a warm meal. There will be time for talk later."

Inside the shack Aerial dished up three piping hot bowls of home-made soup from the large crock simmering over the fireplace. He spread an old tattered blanket on the floor. The kids sat cross-legged eating their soup. The man sat down in a rickety wooden rocking chair. Slowly he began to speak while the soup warmed their insides.

"I've lived in Virlingreal all my life. But I've lived here in this shack only a short time. My name is Aerial. Have you met the others?"

"We've seen the children," replied Lindsey.

"Then you know?"

"Know, sir?"

A puzzled look crossed Aerial's face.

"You don't need to pretend."

Aerial stood up from the rocking chair and walked over to a small wooden table with four chairs pushed underneath it.

"Something had to be done." H sat down, then looked up at the girl.

"It was getting too complicated."

"We need to know about the V-bug and the thinking."

Aerial chucked at the girl's words.

"There isn't much to know," he said glancing toward the overstuffed bookshelves against the back wall of the little cabin. He cleared his throat. Then quickly looked away.

"What about those books?"

"Yes, what of them?"

"My father has books like that." Pat's eyes were glued to the bookshelves.

"Those books are not for you."

"But–"

"There are things best left alone," Aerial replied quickly interrupting the boy.

"What things?"

Aerial was becoming agitated with the boy's persistence. He drew a slow breath and stared at the boy.

"Do you know anything about dreams?"

"My history teacher thinks so."

Mike chuckled at Pat's reply. Aerial's head instantly jerked in Mike's direction.

"We need to know everything. You must help us," said Lindsey adamantly.

Aerial looked back at the girl. He seemed surprised by her remark. He stood pushing his chair back away from the table, then moved to the far side of the room in front of the fireplace. He peered deep into the flames. Suddenly, he turned.

"I've decided to trust you."

He hesitated glancing toward the boys. Then he cleared his throat and continued speaking.

"My solitude is my treasure. In the woods I take late evening walks. Now I will take you back in time. It all started three months ago. It was then I quite accidentally happened upon them– the strangers. They were studying our land, gathering samples of our vegetation and soil and storing them in metallic containers. I followed at a safe distance. And then–"

Aerial stopped. There was a long pause as he again gazed deeply into the fire. Then he reached back without turning and grabbed a chair pulling it forward as if to steady himself.

"I couldn't take my eyes off it," he said as he lowered himself into the chair. His eyes widened as he said it.

"A space vessel was all I could think." He looked directly at Pat.

"Was I having an encounter with aliens?"

Pat didn't move a muscle as Aerial stared directly at him, but he did wonder if the man could hear the thumping sound. He placed his hand on his chest as if he was trying to stop it, but he knew he couldn't.

There wasn't much that scared the boy other than what you have already heard many times earlier in this story. He was older now and probably could handle it better. But he never forgot– and probably never would– that day at Cyberland. He was seven at the time. He had lied about his age. Later that day he swore he'd never lie again.

He knew his father was close by. But it didn't seem to matter this time. Nothing mattered this time. Whatever he tried to do he just couldn't stop the feeling. He heard the scream. It didn't even sound like his own voice, but he knew it was.

"Close your eyes Pat and keep them closed," his father kept repeating.

"Tell yourself it's not real."

He closed his eyes and said it now. This time his heartbeat slowed, something he couldn't make happen that day in Cyberland.

"I was never a believer. It turned out it wasn't a space vessel at all. Just a window."

Pat squinted.

"You mean the kind you look out?" Aerial chuckled.

"No. The kind you look in. And every request must first be approved. Do you know about the Controllers?"

Pat nodded.

"A little." Then he glanced toward his sister.

"Don't believe everything you hear about them." Aerial hesitated. "But I can tell you one thing for sure." He looked up from his chair.

"They think they know everything, but they're wrong."

"Who thinks they know everything?" responded the girl.

"The Controllers." He was looking at the ceiling now.

"I returned only once to that window. I had been visiting my wife and daughter. They live in the mountains." He looked down shaking his head.

"I suppose it was stupid of me to do what I did. As you probably know Components are supposed to just follow the Controller's orders. But blindly following orders was never something I was good at."

He lowered his voice.

"I slipped right through. They never saw me, or so I thought then."

He quickly glanced out the window in his shack.

"When I returned to my shack I noticed them. I figured I didn't have much time. That night I went to bed expecting to never awake. But in the morning I felt just fine so I slipped into town. It was a Thursday. The night of the local Controllers town hall meeting. Down a back alley I pried open a window. Stretching on my toes and pressing my ear close, I heard just enough about their latest war plans."

Aerial looked at Mike taking a long pause before continuing.

"Do you know anything about war?"

He glanced at Lindsey, and then Pat.

"What do any of you know about war?"

No one responded.

"It won't be pretty if we let them get away with it. War is all they seem to understand."

Aerial quickly ripped open the front of his shirt. Pat shielded his eyes looking away, but Mike didn't. In fact, Mike couldn't stop himself from staring directly at the long black scar down the front of Aerial's chest.

"If it happens to you, you can forget about the Olympics."

Pat turned, glancing at his friend, wondering what Mike was thinking. His friend's eyes looked different now and were glued to Aerial's chest. It almost didn't look like Mike, at least in the face, but Pat knew it was. He could never mistake his best friend. The boy who lived just a few doors down the street all his life. The one with the unshakeable belief in himself. But something strange was happening now. It was almost like someone or something was taking control of Mike.

Was it the thought of war or was it something about this strange place? Pat knew Mike had never been involved in a real war. He knew they all had heard about wars and the effects wars have on people like Mike's father. Mike's father had talked to him about it, just like Pat's dad had explained the effect of war on those who lived through it. They had talked about what it was like to lose a friend in a war. But war was something very distant to Pat and Mike.

Real wars hadn't happened in their lifetimes. War was something you watched on television, or played in your backyard when you were a kid. With that kind of war when you got tired you just went home and your mother yelled at you and told you to wash up for dinner. That was war to Pat and Mike. But Aerial was talking about something else.

Lindsey interrupted breaking the tension.

"Listen guys. We've faced tough challenges before."

Pat stared at his sister. What in God's name was she talking about?

He thought back to the time when Mike was just four years old and alone on Crescent Hill one block over from Cherry Street. His friend had told him about it later. Pat wished he had gone with him that day.

He recalled looking down at the two shiny white teeth Mike proudly held in the palm of his hand when he got back. He was proud of the big hole in his smile too. It was the result of Mike listening to his father's early advice in preparing him to become a great downhill skier.

"Go fast, take chances," Roger would often tell his son.

Pat's best friend had faced challenges preparing for the Olympics, but Aerial was talking about something else.

"What can you tell us about the strangers and what does it have to do with war?" Pat asked.

"I have three of their books," replied Aerial.

He pointed to the bottom corner of his bookshelf. Pat's eyes locked on the cover of one book. It was a book he had seen before.

In small print under the words "Integrating CRISPR Technology with Intelligent Robots," it said, "by Fred E. McMichaels."

On the bottom shelf below the book by his father crumpled in the corner was a yellowing torn page from an old issue of the Virlingreal Gazette. Circled in bright red ink were the words, "ALRCs Still Missing."

Chapter Thirteen – Thinking better

The idea of artificial intelligence, meaning intelligence demonstrated by machines, had been around almost as long as computer technology. But most of the AI research prior to Fred's project had led to disappointing results due largely to the exaggerated claims of how computers could think faster and better than humans. The faster part was undeniable. It was the better part that kept stumping the researchers.

What does it mean to think better? And how do you teach kids to think better so they can make better decisions? This had been the focus of Fred's secret project at the Jefferson Lab.

The idea was to create realistic environments for learning that challenged students by placing them in real-life situations. The real-life situation part was the discriminator that Fred used to get the funding for his project approved by the government.

In the past higher education institutions had often used classroom scenarios with role playing exercises to help students learn. But these made-up situations too often failed to provide the types of challenges most often faced in the real world.

The real break-throughs with artificial intelligence started happening a few years before 2020 and it happened coincidental with the advent of social media, the virtual emersion gaming craze and the internet of things. The internet of things, known as IOT, is the modern world of interconnected humans and devices made possible through software and sensors. But most of the effort before Fred's project focused on commercial products for consumers interested in being entertained.

Fred had a vision for a much greater use of the technology in the education field, but to achieve his vision he knew there was one big nut he had to crack and that was how to integrate artificial intelligence, virtual reality, and reality.

With the fast-paced changes of the early twenty-first century the higher education institutions weren't keeping pace and more and more kids were beginning to question the value of spending hundreds of thousands of dollars and starting their lives with big debts for a college degree that was providing less and less real value in the modern world.

Fred was convinced he had the answer to this dilemma in what he called his "hybrid virtual-reality-reality" engine, or HVRR for short. The HVRR engine was based on a similar idea to work-study programs that had been around for years where college kids experience the real world intermixed with semesters of course work.

But there were two big differences with Fred's HVRR engine. First, the program could learn and re-program itself based on what it learned. And second, Fred had figured out how to integrate AI, CRISPR and IOT. This was the breakthrough Fred needed to make his HVRR engine a true innovation that could improve the way people think.

The idea of a computer program re-programming itself as it learned wasn't new, but Fred was the first researcher to apply the idea in the education field through his ALRCs.

But there was a problem. The ALRCs were proving to be too good. And when the guys in Washington got wind of what Fred was doing, they decided to shut the project down because it might just put the higher education institutions out of work and that could mean huge layoffs in the education field and a major economic recession. In Washington– as in business—it's all about the money!

But by the time Washington learned what Fred was doing, what they didn't know was that it might already have been too late to stop what Fred had started. That's because a few of Fred's renegade ALRCs got even smarter than Fred thought they could, and they decided to take control and just tell the kids what to do rather than teach them how to solve their own problems through better thinking. And that's when all hell started to break loose!

Chapter Fourteen – Thinking too much

"Come here."

Aerial stood close to the window in the front of his shack looking down the road. Lindsey rose from the blanket Aerial had laid out on the floor. Her bones felt stiff from all the walking they'd been doing that day. She was surprised given the shape she was in from basketball, but she just figured running up and down a basketball floor uses different muscle groups than walking for hours in a strange land.

"Look at them." Aerial pointed.

"It was Friday when I first noticed. I didn't think much of it."

He squinted as he peered out the window.

"How long does it take a Component to fix a pothole in Farthington?"

"We don't have Components in Farthington," replied Lindsey.

"But my father says it takes city workers about two and a half years."

Aerial had a puzzled look on his face as he turned and looked at the girl.

"They've been at it three days. Around here a Component can fix a pothole in an afternoon, if he puts his limited mind to it."

He looked down rubbing his chin.

"Something isn't right."

"Aerial, I have an idea," said Lindsey.

"I'm all ears," replied Aerial.

"We know the guys in charge gave the kids CRISPR to get them to do what they want here in Virlingreal. Right? "

"Aerial shook his head in agreement."

"Couldn't we sneak into the Controller's headquarters and replace the CRISPR formula they are using on the kids with our own reprogrammed CRISPR formula that will help kids think on their own again?"

Aerial hesitated pondering the idea a bit before responding to the girl.

"How would we figure out how to program the CRISPR?"

"I read an article on the internet that explained how to program CRISPR and they even give you step by step instructions when you purchase CRISPR right on Amazon.com."

Aerial hesitated again, rubbing his chin.

"That sounds like an interesting idea. But if I'm seen leaving, especially with strangers–" He hesitated once more.

"Worse yet, if I get a call and don't respond–" Aerial hesitated again, only this time something seemed to be going wrong inside of him as he started shaking his head back and forth, again and again, faster and faster.

Then he grabbed hold of his head and the shaking slowed enough for him to respond.

"I'm sorry. I cannot help you. I just ran through the possibilities in my head and it started to overload my circuits. It would be just too risky."

We need Aerial on this team thought Lindsey. We will need his experience and his knowledge of how things work in this strange land. He was peering out the window in the front of his shack again.

"Aerial, what exactly would happen if a Controller called and you didn't respond?"

"A report would instantly be dispatched to the Executive Kernel. He's the top guy in charge. And once he's in the loop I'll be in hot water for sure."

Aerial hesitated once again. Then he turned away from the window and took a step back.

"And it wouldn't be the first time." His eyes peered downward.

"What do you mean?" Slowly, he raised his head.

"I– I've been caught before, sneaking off to the mountains to visit my family. My wife– she's a good person– but the old shack never suited her. She lives in the mountains where life runs at a bit of a slower pace."

"It must be hard with your wife and daughter so far away."

"The distance isn't a problem. It's time that we keep running out of." A puzzled look came over his face.

"What is it, Aerial?"

"Oh nothing, it's just that–" He hesitated again.

"Just that what?"

"Time. I was just thinking–" Aerial stopped again in the middle of his sentence. Then he started to mumble. He was acting incoherent.

"What is it, Aerial?" she persisted.

"It was a long time ago. Late one night. I was alone."

"Did something happen?"

"They came." Aerial's eyes were acting strange.

"Who came, Aerial?"

"The bad boys."

He started to mumble incoherently again as he pointed toward the window. Lindsey glanced at her brother. His face was bright red and his jaw had dropped wide open. Then she turned back looking again at Aerial.

"What are you trying to tell us, Aerial?"

"Time," he mumbled.

"We can easily get out of sync here in Virlingreal and then things don't work so well."

He stared at the wall on the far side of the room.

"What about time?" she asked again. His mouth was open, but it had stopped moving for a few moments. Then he managed to shut it as he reached up scratching his head.

"Forget it. It's too complicated," he added.

"We don't mind complications," insisted the girl. "Tell us more about the Controllers. When they call what do they want from you? And what would the Executive Kernel do once he found out you weren't responding?"

"The Executive Kernel monitors the duty roster and that is where they keep their CRISPR formula. The duty roster contains the daily list of things to do and anything else they need to carry out their daily tasks."

"Can we get to it? Can we change it?" The girl started rattling off questions without waiting for answers.

Pat interrupted,

"But even if we can modify the CRISPR formula to help the kids, won't the Controllers eventually catch on and try to change it back?"

It was a good question. It showed that Pat was really thinking through this problem.

Then he turned and looked at Aerial.

"Aerial, couldn't we also use CRISPR to help the guys on top understand why they need to let the kids think and learn?"

"Slow down." Aerial shook his head.

"This is crazy. You know it, don't you?" His eyes panned his three young visitors.

"No. I suppose you don't." He looked away.

"If we did modify the CRISPR they are giving to the kids, and—going along with Pat's idea—if we also modified the Controller's orders using CRISPR, then at least we'd stand a fighting chance. But we would need to think through every step. My God! I don't believe we're actually talking about this.

But if we did modify those files our only hope of surviving would be to catch a fast bus to the window—and now I'm not talking about the window in my shack—but the window near the back door of the Kernel's place. We could use that window to get out of Virlingreal before they catch us."

Aerial's head jerked back. Then he took two more quick steps back.

"Our one hope that makes me think this could work is that Controllers aren't really that smart.

In fact, they aren't even as smart as most Components. They have limited brain power and just follow the orders in the duty roster without much thinking. If we did succeed in making these changes and got out of Virlingreal in time, then everyone would stand a fighting chance of thinking better on their own including the controllers and the guys at the top."

But then Aerial stopped talking and put his left hand over his mouth. His head and shoulders both started to droop.

All of a sudden he began to look pale and haggard. He was standing in his shack looking as if he was lost. And just then his head began to shake uncontrollably.

He then took a deep breath as if he was trying to gather himself. Then he peered down at the filth on the floor.

"But breaking into the kernel's place and modifying the duty roster–" He hesitated once more. "A sane person would haul you away just for thinking it. We'll need to study every inch of the place. Expect trouble at every turn. One wrong move and–" He stopped again and started shaking his head back and forth in a slow deliberate way.

Lindsey had no clue why Aerial seemed to be so worried. She had no idea what was going on inside his head. She didn't know that Aerial was trying to think about every little thing that might go wrong and every time he did this much thinking it was coming close to overloading his circuits again.

He was trying to figure out all the things he would need to keep in his mind all at once when they would go on this challenging mission. And what if his thoughts became jumbled? What if he couldn't think fast enough? What if he froze at just the wrong time?

Aerial knew more than anyone what went on in every inch of the kernel's place. He knew every little thing that might go wrong. He knew every reason not to do it. He stood in his disheveled shack thinking about his life and what he had let it become. He had been taking his evening walks and thinking. Just thinking.

He now was coming to the realization that, despite all his thinking, he had allowed himself to stop thinking big and taking risks like he used to when he was young. While the idea of breaking into the kernel's place scared him to death it was also exhilarating to him and that feeling was something he had not felt for a long time.

He turned and looked at his three visitors, took a deep breath to calm himself and said,

"We're going to do it and I am not going to worry anymore about all the things that might go wrong."

He took one more deep breath, and then let it out and said,

"Sometimes you can think too much."

Chapter Fifteen – Fast rides

"We haven't a moment to lose."

Aerial looked down at the large brown and wooden trunk pushed against the far wall beside the fireplace. He reached to open it. He hesitated catching sight of Pat out of the corner of his eye. He shook his head. Then he opened the trunk and reached inside. Slowly he removed three old, but well cared for, books. They were wrapped in soft blue cloth.

"We don't outnumber them, but we can certainly outsmart them."

He rubbed his chin.

"It's a good distance from the kernel's place to our escape window. We'll need to take a bus. But we can walk from my shack to the kernel's place as long as we go at night when its dark and use camouflage so we're not noticed."

He shook his head again.

"If you hear alarms go off, don't even bother to run. Now get some rest. We go tonight."

For the next few moments no one spoke. Mike's mind was wandering. If he made it at skiing, he'd live like a king. He had it all figured out. You had to be smart or real good. The boy's goal was to become the best he could at skiing, and he figured everything else would take care of itself. But Aerial didn't fit the pattern.

"How come you live in a shack?"

"Pardon me?"

"I said how come you live in a run down one room dirty old shack with a front yard full of mud? If you're so smart, how come you're not doing a little better."

"Doing a little better?" retorted Aerial.

"Yea, like running the place. Like having servants. Like eating whatever and whenever you want."

Pat chucked at his friend's words. He knew Mike wasn't trying to be mean. He knew his friend didn't think any less of Aerial for it. It just didn't make sense to him and he wanted to know more.

"Why, Aerial?" he persisted.

"I told you before, don't try to understand everything at once."

Then he blew out the flame in the lamp. They laid on the tattered blanket in the middle of the cabin floor. No words were spoken, but no one slept. Shadows from the fireplace danced across the wall. Hearts thumped. Minds raced. Only time was moving slowly now.

Pat thought of his mother and his father. Been two days. Just two days. The boy was missing his mother. Just a bit. It wasn't anything he couldn't handle. He didn't need her for anything in particular. He just missed that feeling– knowing she was close. Just in case.

Better think about something else, he thought to himself. I'm sixteen. Sixteen. He looked at Mike. They hadn't spent this much time together since the summer of the tunnel. That summer was the last time Pat could recall when he had all the time in the world. It was the way he thought things were supposed to be. The way they would always be. But at that moment in the solitude of the night Pat's mind was in a different time. A time when less important things mattered.

Sleepovers, he thought. How long has it been? Sleepovers used to scare Mike. Pat recalled how he would have to tell his friend to shut his eyes and when he opened them again it would be a different time and he could go home. Pat shut his eyes now, and the darkness soon came, and then it was time.

They dressed in black smearing dried mud gathered from the front yard on their faces. Out the backdoor they slipped eluding the dozing city components. Through the countryside they moved swiftly with Aerial leading the way.

"Keep low and close," said Aerial.

In the darkness they could see only a few feet in front. It turned out to be a longer and more difficult walk to the kernel's place than Aerial indicated. Pat was tiring as they climbed a long hill, but he refused to let the others know. They crested a hill and Pat looked back. The view reminded him of a place near his home where he had hiked with his father and sister.

"Keep moving," said Aerial as they approached the kernel's castle. A treacherous section of Snake River surrounded it.

"Don't get too close. It's for unwelcome guests."

"You mean like us?" quipped Pat. Aerial nodded.

"Yes, like us."

Across a narrow footbridge five hundred feet above the river they followed Aerial in single file.

"It leads directly to the kernel's back door." Aerial muffled his voice.

"The bridge is weak. We must each cross alone."

Aerial went first. Mike followed. Pat turned and looked at his sister. Five-hundred feet, he thought. He shook his head. She had broken into a cold sweat. It wasn't the first time it had gotten to her. There wasn't much that scared Pat's sister– not snakes, not bugs, not even aliens. But there had always been something about height.

Suddenly, Pat reached out and grabbed his sister. He shook her firmly at the shoulders. And this was quite unusual for the boy because, in general, he didn't like touching his sister at all.

"Linz, you've got to take hold of yourself. Just do it!"

He was looking at her squarely in the eyes. A dazed confused look had come over her. She didn't seem to understand him or be quite herself. He crossed the bridge, then quickly looked back. She wasn't in sight. The thought of actually losing his sister jolted him. He started to tremble.

Pat's big sister Lindsey had studied hard in school. She had a terrific memory. She could recall detailed facts which she adeptly pulled from her brain at just the right time. Pat so admired his sister's tenacity for learning that he had long ago decided it was best to just let her do most of the thinking. No sense having them both rack their brains, he figured.

But now she wasn't there, and what a time to lose her! He couldn't go back and he couldn't wait any longer. What would it mean to the boy to go on without his big sister? Better not think about it now, he thought to himself. Better just put it out of my mind and move on.

Only a few steps from the back door, they crouched low in the brush.

"That's it." Aerial pointed. Suddenly, his face turned white.

"How stupid of me!" he scolded himself.

Then he quickly opened his mouth, but at first no words came out. Pat stared at him wondering if his mind had stopped. And what if it did stop? What if Aerial's mind froze at just the wrong time? Pat shook his head. He didn't want to think any more about that either.

"They've updated their operating system," said Aerial.

Pat didn't know exactly what it meant, but he had an idea. He knew that engineers were always fiddling with the software and that could mean you should expect the unexpected.

"See those dogs?" Aerial pointed, then shook his head.

"It's too risky with those animals nosing around. We'll need to switch to the backup plan."

Aerial tilted his head. Noises were coming from down near the river. The dogs were into a chase.

"Keep low, " warned Aerial.

A faint figure appeared in the distance. It was a young woman. She was running at full speed. And she was dripping wet.

"It's Lindsey!" cried Pat. The girl ducked behind the bushes as the watchdogs streaked by. She hadn't yet caught her breath, but Aerial just stared.

The boy knew his sister better than anyone. He knew she was a strong swimmer and an outstanding runner. A raging river and trained dogs were no match for her– at least at ground level.

Aerial shook his head. Two feats he had never before seen and both accomplished by the same person on the same day.

"The boys down at the barber shop will never believe this one," he mused to himself.

A sleek grey bus approached the castle. Pat crouched low along the side of the road. He was thinking about his sister. He was proud of her.

"Pat! Wake up!" It was Aerial yelling at him now. The boy's head jerked back. He jumped into the road frantically waving his arms. The bus screeched to a halt.

"Out of the way!" screamed the driver. "Nothing must stop the kernel's mail!"

"You'll never make it!" replied Pat.

"There's a swarm of P-bugs just around the bend!"

P-bugs were different from V-bugs and everyone in Virlingreal knew the difference.

We have already explained V-bugs. P-bugs, unlike V-bugs, could attack anyone at anytime in Virlingreal. Not just the kids. And when they hit the effects could range from minor problems to causing complete havoc to the whole state of Virlingreal. They had even been known to bring the whole city to a complete standstill.

The bus driver squinted.

"What do you want me to do?"

"Just stay cool. We're working the problem. The line should be clear soon."

As Pat and the bus driver conversed about the weather, Aerial slipped onto the back of the bus and made the changes to the CRISPR formula and placed a request for a high priority bus.

"All clear. Better step on it."

Along the edge of the road they sat, legs crossed and arms folded, just as Aerial had explained how they needed to in order to be prepared for what was going to happen next.

"Once those messages are decoded we'll be off in a flash. Just hang on tight," said Aerial.

Pat had always liked fast rides. He loved the feeling of the wind blowing through his hair, but that was back in his younger days when he had hair. He loved to just let go.

Suddenly, without any notice, something very bad happened. The boy reached up, but it was too late. He didn't have a chance to stop it from blowing off his head. He turned watching his Atlanta Braves baseball cap blow slowly away. He watched it go as far as he could until it was completely out of sight.

He could have let himself feel bad about it. That hat was important to him. It was his favorite baseball team. He had owned that hat since he was seven.

Whenever something good happened to the boy– it seemed– something bad happened soon after. He still wanted to let go. He wanted to completely enjoy the ride. And the speed. But this time he just couldn't make himself forget completely about that hat.

He looked at Mike. Ever since skiing had taken over his friend's life, Mike had all the answers. It had been different when they were younger. But still Pat could tell when something was bothering his friend. Like now, and Pat could sense it just by looking at Mike's face.

The boy was slipping and it made no sense. It seemed like everything that was happening in this strange land made no sense. Mike was strong. Pat wanted desperately to help his friend. He wanted to scream out at the top of his lungs to help his friend. There was nothing Pat wanted more at that moment in time than to tell his friend he could do it—to give him encouragement and positive feedback. To tell him to just hang on for a little longer and then everything would be alright.

But for some unexplainable reason– at that very moment– Pat couldn't get his mouth to open. His best friend was in serious trouble. He needed Pat maybe more than he ever needed him before, and at that very moment in time Pat couldn't get his mouth to open so he could help his best friend.

Mike's left hand had slipped completely off the bus. Rapidly he was losing his grip with his right. Pat's head turned away. He didn't do it on purpose. It just turned as if it had a mind of its own. He heard a scream. He didn't want to look, but he made himself look. And what he saw when he made himself look he swore he'd never forget no matter how long his life went on.

It was a face. The face of someone he had known all his life. Someone he knew Mike North outweighed by sixty pounds. And she was holding onto Pat's friend with a single hand while holding the speeding grey bus with the other. It didn't seem real, but it was as real as everything else in this story.

For years Lindsey had worked diligently to strengthen key muscle groups in her forearm and wrist. She had done the exercises primarily to help with her dribbling. Her goal was complete finger-tip control. She had also worked on her leg muscles for quick response on defense and to improve her rebounding skills.

Lindsey understood the value of training. But there was a limit to how far she would go, even for basketball. She had watched other woman working out with free-weights at the University and had decided she would never let herself look that way. Her coach said it would improve her rebounding, and give her the strength to push the bigger girls around on the inside. But being pushy wasn't Lindsey's style.

Her edge was quickness and her ability to out-think the competition. But to make the coach happy she had agreed to give free-weights a try and when she did she had found she couldn't get a hundred pounds off the ground. And that was using both arms.

The week before this whole adventure started Pat had been sitting in the waiting room at his dentist's office. He had been reading a magazine article about superhuman feats. The article said that each person has a drive deep inside them. A drive to make the world agree with what they believed. For hundreds of years medical doctors believed no human could run a mile in less than four minutes. One medical doctor believed differently. On May 6, 1954, Roger Bannister, a British born physician and runner, stepped to the starting line in a mile race in Oxford, England. Less than four minutes later he crossed the finish line breaking the world record. News flashed around the world. Two months later John Landy, an Australian athlete, stepped to the starting line in the race in which he would break Bannister's brief record.

"Run as fast as you can," cried Aerial as the bus screeched to a halt. Down a hill they streaked.

"Quick, in here." Aerial pointed to a small cave tucked out of sight behind three oversized grey boulders.

"Keep very still." He raised a single finger to his lip.

Only the sound of pounding hearts could be heard. Cautiously, Aerial moved to the front of the cave. He peered beyond the rocks.

"We may have caused side-effects," he said in a low voice.

He looked at Mike.

"Especially with you hanging on that way. They'll be checking it out tonight. If we're lucky, they'll decide it was just a transient P-Bug."

"Are we near the window?" asked Lindsey.

"Yes. It's just beyond the rocks, but don't get curious. It's too risky. Now get some rest. Tomorrow things only get tougher."

Pat stared at Aerial. He took a deep breath.

Tomorrow, he thought, things only get tougher! Better not think about it anymore today.

Chapter Sixteen – A different drug

How many lives do you think you have? If you had more than one, would you live your current one differently? Sometimes we humans can't get out of our heads thoughts about what if things had gone differently in our life. But if you could go back and live another version of your life, do you think you would really live it differently?

Fred's discovery of his HVRR engine was ingenious, but none of the other AI researchers could see what was right in front of Fred's face when he discovered it. What Fred understood was that we need to let computers do what computers do best, like simple repetitive tasks, and let humans do what humans do best, like innovative thinking and problem-solving. And most important Fred understood how to go about blending AI, CRISPR and just the right amount of methylation.

But with Fred's discovery everything didn't go so smoothly. Fred expected his discovery would give people more time to do the important things that humans should be doing.

But when the people found that they had more time, they filled their time with more repetitive non-innovative tasks like playing games on their devices and making comments on their social media sites.

And then more and more people started walking around completely plugged in, never talking directly to other human beings except through their electronic devices. So, the government picked up on this realizing that social media could be used like a drug to get the people to do what they wanted.

Any thoughts that didn't align with what the government wanted the people to believe were referred to as "fake news." And the government thus brainwashed as many people as they could into believing whatever they wanted them to believe and into doing whatever they wanted them to do, just by repeating stuff over and over, whether it was true or not.

And thus, the "guys on top" took control ensuring all the people would hear and see and believe and do just what they wanted them to hear and see and believe and do.

Chapter Seventeen – One last bug

The children had been missing for three days.

"Fred, why don't you go to work?"

"The Norths will be home today," replied Fred. A strained look appeared on his face.

"Don't worry, dear. I'll handle it." His wife smiled.

There were two entrances leading into the Jefferson Lab. Those who needed to know knew about the second one. Fred flashed his badge at the second entrance. He opened his briefcase. Robert, the guard, nodded.

"Have a good weekend, machine?"

Robert referred to Fred as "the machine" in deference to Fred's dedication to running. Six days a week. Thursdays off until his dedication became an obsession and the regular Thursdays off became a day off every few months and only when Fred felt an injury coming on.

"Did a fifteen miler on Saturday," replied Fred.

It was a lie, but Fred didn't want to alert security that anything unusual might be going on. He moved past the guard and the surveillance cameras down a long narrow hall leading to a massive iron door. He had taken this same walk every workday for the past seven years. Each time it reminded him of George Orwell's futuristic novel of years past. He fumbled at the door sliding his badge into the scanner and keying in his security code. The green light blinked. The door drew open. In his office he set his briefcase down on his desk. He glanced at his calendar.

"Oh no! How could I have forgotten!"

Quickly he picked up the phone entering a four digit extension.

"C'mon...C'mon," he uttered impatiently to himself.

He tapped his fingers on the desk with his right hand as he held the phone to his ear with his left.

"Meg? Fred. What's the status?"

Meg Savitch was an engineer at the Jefferson Lab. She was scheduled to lead a critical demonstration for the customer at nine o'clock that morning. It was already eight-forty-five. The demonstration had completely slipped Fred's mind.

"Worked all weekend on the last few bugs. Got my fingers crossed," replied Meg.

Meg Savitch had recently made a career change. She was now an education specialist. The change had not been easy. Due to security she was not permitted to discuss her work with her husband Bill. Six months earlier Bill was let go from his company. He had been with Triple-A Instruments over thirty years.

Meg and Bill had two sons, Ryan and Jesse. Jesse had struggled through every year of his schooling and at fourteen it wasn't getting easier for him. Meg had been working with Fred on this secret project for the past three years. She hoped that one day the results of her work might help her son.

Fred was familiar with the phrase "last few bugs." It wasn't what he wanted to hear. But this demonstration had to go on at nine o'clock. He hung up the phone. Instantly, it rang. Vice-President Washburn from the Jefferson Lab and three government customers were on their way to the demonstration room.

Fred's forehead began to sweat. He hung up the phone again. Only a few weeks earlier everything had been going smoothly. Then the newspaper got hold of the big two billion dollar story. That's when

Washington started nosing around and asking questions– tough questions.

Fred sighed. He glanced at the article laying on the side of his desk. The words, "nothing to show for it," jumped out at him. He shook his head and crossed his fingers. Then he headed down the hall to the demonstration room.

On the outside he was a picture of confidence. On the inside his insides were feeling like jello. He took a deep breath and entered the room.

"Good morning, Jason. Hello, Frank. How's your boy's soccer season coming, Tom?"

Fred's out-going style wasn't something that came natural to him. But times had changed and so had Fred.

"Gentlemen, please be seated. It gives me great pleasure this morning to introduce you to Meg Savitch. Meg is one of our top education specialists here at Jefferson. She will be leading you through today's demonstration."

"Thank you, Fred. Good morning. For those of you who don't know me, I've been working on this project for over three years."

Meg smiled.

"We begin by initializing the system."

It was back in 2015 when the President and Congress had secretly agreed to fund this latest education project. Few details were known to the public. Lenny was a top engineer at the Lab. He was sitting in the back of the room. He understood the system better than anyone. That is, anyone except Maynard Jackson. Earlier that morning the system had been acting strangely. Lenny didn't know why. He wanted to call the demonstration off.

"The software you are about to see is the result of years of cognitive research here at Jefferson into how we can best prepare our children for the future challenges they are certain to face. Please direct your attention to the large screen in the front of the room."

She's got them in the palm of her hand, thought Fred. His tense stomach began to calm. Just then a message flashed across the bottom of the screen. Fred squinted.

"Oh no!" Fred looked at Lenny just as an alarm sounded. Then another message flashed in large red letters.

"RED ALERT!– SYSTEM ILLEGALLY ENTERED!"

The words repeated through the audio system, as Lenny sat back in his chair. He wasn't surprised, but he was a bit puzzled. He had never heard or seen that exact message before. The system was hung in a tight loop, and with each iteration Fred's throat tightened a little more too.

"Meeting at eleven. My office!" said the Vice-President sternly. He walked out of the room.

"Meg, get the team going on this top priority!" demanded Fred.

"Ok, but I have to leave at two-thirty today."

Fred glanced at the screen. Suddenly, his face turned stone-white.

"What is it, Fred?" Slowly, he turned and looked at her.

"Could it be–" He stopped in the middle of his sentence.

"Could it be what, Fred?"

"Just find that bug!" It was all he said.

Meg Savich enjoyed her work at the lab. She wanted what she did to count. What she was doing now could count a lot, she thought. She stood in the demonstration room thinking about breakfast that morning. She recalled looking across the kitchen table at her husband Bill. She had wanted desperately to tell him right then how what they were doing could help their son, Jesse. She had wanted to tell him a hundred times before. Tonight would be the night, she had thought when she got up that morning. She turned and looked at the large screen in the front of the room.

"One last bug." She mumbled it under her breath.

"There's always one last bug."

Chapter Eighteen – A crazy dream

Pat was rubbing his hands trying to keep warm as he sat close to the fire.

"Aerial, why do the kids near the river live that way?"

"It wasn't something they chose," replied Aerial.

"They are just dealing with a bad situation the best they can."

"It isn't right," said Pat. He pulled his hands back from the fire.

"You don't know the full story. I used to live in the mountains with my wife and daughter. Then I caught a different kind of bug. The kind that stays with you no matter what you do or where you go." Aerial paused.

Pat looked at Lindsey and Mike. They had fallen asleep.

"When I came to Swampy Pond my family stayed in the mountains." Aerial stopped for a moment looking away from the fire into the darkness, and then he continued.

"My daughter Erica spent two summers with me. But she needed to get back to her schooling and her friends and people her own age."

"Mr. Osgood, my history teacher where I go to school, said they're teaching us all the wrong stuff in school today."

Aerial looked at the boy.

"I think you're learning just what you need right now."

Pat shrugged. Aerial tilted his head quizzically.

"What are you looking for?"

"I don't know. But I think I'll know it when I find it."

Aerial smile. It was the first time Pat saw him smile and just then Pat reached out to touch his new friend. But when Pat's hand reached Aerial's shoulder it didn't stop. It kept going right through Aerial's shoulder completely disappearing!

The sight of it horrified Pat. Aerial's body began to shake and so did Pat's. And at that moment in time there was only a single thought in Pat's head and it was the only thought that made any sense at all to the boy–

If I could just get my body moving right now I would certainly fall from my bed and wake up from this crazy dream.

And so, he tried to move. But trying to move only caused his body to shake more and the more Pat's body shook the more Aerial's body shook too.

In fact, Aerial's body was shaking from his neck to his toes and his eyes were rolling in and out of his head.

"Oh boy, look what I did now!" exclaimed Pat.

"Aerial, what can I do?" he cried.

Aerial didn't respond. He was clasping his head with both his hands. He fell to the ground. Sounds were coming from his mouth, but it sounded like his mouth wasn't connected to his brain. Pat took a deep breath. He told himself to keep calm.

"I must have triggered a bug," he said to himself. He looked to see if Aerial had a restart button, but he couldn't find one. Slowly Aerial's body calmed down on its own.

"Pat, never touch me that way again. It fouls up my insides."

The boy wasn't trying to be bad. He wasn't trying to cause anything bad to happen to Aerial. He just wanted at that moment to be close. Being close didn't come easy to the boy. Sports came easy. With sports Pat knew what to do. He didn't need anyone to tell him. He just knew.

But talking about important things was different. And he wanted to talk. He wanted to talk about the bus ride and about losing his hat. He wanted to talk about Mike, his best friend who he knew he would soon not see again for a very long time. He wanted to talk about all the crazy things he had been feeling over the last few days. And he wanted to talk about things he thought were important that he didn't understand.

One of those things he didn't understand was about his grandfather. He had died before Pat was born, but the boy had heard stories about him from his father.

"I was very young when it happened." Fred had paused for a long moment before telling his son this story.

"We were in the family Plymouth. I recall that car as if I was riding in it yesterday. It was green with a big bumper. I'll never forget that car." He smiled at Pat.

"We had stopped for a red light. My father was driving. We were in downtown Farthington. I looked out the window and saw a man I did not know stumble. Then he fell to the ground.

I didn't think much of it, but apparently my father did. He didn't say anything to me. He just pulled the car over and got out. He seemed to be gone forever and then I heard the back door open and close and some words I couldn't make out. When he got back in the front seat and started driving again I kept looking at him, but he didn't look at me or say anything. I thought something had flipped inside his head.

I didn't know where we were going. I was afraid to look in the backseat. I'll never forget the smell. It stayed in the car for days. Two people watched us when he made the man drink three cups of coffee at Hick's Diner. They were sitting at the counter. He didn't want the coffee and he was getting loud, but my father made him drink it. I felt better when we got out of there. I just wanted to go home, but we didn't go home cause my father had some money.

I could see it bulging out the side of his pants. My father never carried a wallet. It was the most money I ever saw at one time. He pulled it out when he paid for the man's suit at Foley's Department Store. We didn't talk about it at home. I know mom wanted to ask about the smell, but she never did.

I never saw the man again until my father's funeral. All I could think then was that the drunk was alive and my father was dead. He was wearing the same suit my father bought him."

After telling his son that story Pat and his father talked about dying and having goals in life, and what living was about.

"Always have goals, but never let your goals get in the way of your life," Fred told his son.

Dad, it sounds like you are telling me two conflicting ideas, " Pat told his father.

"No," his father told him. "You need to have goals. Goals give you a reason to live and direction to your life. But never let your goals get in the way of doing what is right, right now. You will have many chances in life. But you only have one chance to do what is right at each moment in your life."

It was cold in the cave and the boy was feeling the cold more now. And he wanted to talk more now, but there was just Aerial and something more important seemed to be occupying Aerial's mind at that moment. He had crawled to the edge of the cave and was peering beyond the rocks.

"Quick, douse the fire!" he whispered. "I should have known better!" Aerial scolded himself.

"What is it?" questioned Pat.

"It's the reflection from our campfire. We've been detected. Gather your gear quickly. There isn't a moment to lose."

But, just as he spoke, a howling wind arose.

"Forget your gear! Save yourself!" cried Aerial.

Lindsey and Mike were awakened to find themselves tumbling out of control directly toward a treacherous cliff near the edge of the window. Pat and Aerial crouched low sheltered by one of the large boulders a few feet from the entrance to the cave. A few moments later the howling wind calmed. Cautiously, Aerial crawled back to the edge and peered beyond the rocks.

"We must head for the mountains while we have the chance."

Pat glanced toward the cliff. He saw nothing and he said nothing. He turned and just followed Aerial and didn't want to think more about what had just happened. For two hours they walked. No words were spoken. They just kept walking and that was fine with Pat. Anything that kept himself moving felt fine to Pat. But then Aerial stopped.

"We must rest." It was all he said.

They had reached the foot of the mountains. Pat looked at Aerial. He closed his eyes. He was exhausted, and wanted right then nothing more than to fall sound asleep so he did not have to think anymore that day. But his mind wouldn't let him.

"Do you know where my sister and friend are?" the boy finally asked.

"They are with the strangers now."

It was all that Aerial said. Pat wanted him to say more. He wanted Aerial to talk to him more about it, to tell him anything. Just to talk, but he didn't. Pat closed his eyes again. But Aerial's words refused to stop echoing in his head.

"They are with the strangers now."

Chapter Nineteen – Deep inside

It was Tuesday morning. Early. Time meant everything. But to Maynard Jackson time had little meaning. Maynard Jackson was an engineer who had just worked through the night. It wasn't unusual at the Jefferson Lab.

"Got to find that bug," he mumbled. It was the only thing on his mind.

"Any clues yet, Maynard?"

"Getting close, Meg. I found some bad data in memory." Maynard scratched his head.

"Now, if I could just figure out why?"

The younger engineers often counted on Maynard. But it wasn't always that way. In his youth computers had been far from Maynard's mind. His first love– and maybe his only real love– was baseball.

Before deciding on a career in software, Maynard had given baseball his best shot. He had played for the Virginia Devils out of the Braves organization. But it had taken five long years of professional baseball before he reached the triple-A level. That summer he had turned twenty-five, and his flaming fastball, which had once earned him the revered reputation as one of the best ever to come out of northern Pennsylvania, was losing its zip.

It wasn't happening the way it was supposed to. Ever since his fifth birthday Maynard had dreamed of nothing but playing in the majors. Now, twenty long years later he was twenty-five, and twenty-five is starting to get old for a ball player who'd been giving it his all for twenty long years.

So, the days of Maynard's fastball had slipped by leaving behind a single lingering question: What does a twenty-five year old pitcher, who couldn't quite just-do-it, do now? He had never considered the question before. Why should he? Maynard Jackson was a ball player.

But now it had reached the time for Maynard to make another decision. And that's what he did. Maynard had gone back to school to become a software engineer. Now twenty-five more years had passed in what seemed like a flash and Maynard was over fifty. But none of that mattered now. He double-clicked the restart button. Then he calmly sat back in his chair.

Pat was lying perfectly still with his eyes closed. He knew his body needed sleep, but his racing mind refused to let it. To make matters worse it was getting even colder in the cave, and Pat was starting to hear a disturbing swooshing sound.

At first he tried to just ignore it, but then it became more than just a sound as he started to feel wet. He opened his eyes and everywhere he looked there was nothing but water. Gushing frigid water rushing through the cave.

Quickly he tried to collect his thoughts, but there just wasn't time to think. The frigid water was becoming colder and stronger and it was starting to move his body without Pat's consent and the force was becoming just too much for the boy to overcome. The water was carrying Pat's body out of the cave and away from the mountains back toward that nightmarish cliff.

He was moving fast now, sliding out of his control down the mountainside. The cold triggered memories inside the boy's head– memories of long ago and a different place. It was a place Pat used to pretend was his own private beach in his own private world.

It was near his maternal grandmother's house. She lived in New

England and he was thinking of one particular day at that beach. He had gone to the beach that day despite his mother's warnings. The cold had never bothered him before– even when it turned his lips blue.

That September day, would be no different, he had thought. He had never felt cold like that day before, nor seen waves act that way. But it wasn't the cold nor the waves that scared him that day in September. That day something felt different and he felt something deep inside that he thought had changed him forever.

He looked down. He saw the cliff. Then he quickly looked up catching sight of a branch of an old oak tree overhanging the cliff. He opened his mouth to yell. He wanted to let Aerial know about the tree and the branch since it was all he could see that might save them from the treacherous cliff. But when he opened his mouth and tried to yell nothing came out. Damn! he thought to himself. It's happening again!

He didn't know what else to do so he did the only thing he thought of which was to jump as high as he could and as he did he was able to grab hold of that overhanging branch. He was now holding on for dear life and as he did he looked down just in time to see what appeared to be Aerial slipping over the edge.

He swung his body in the direction of dry land. Then he let go with a fling landing safely. Instantly he turned, crawling back, and started to look over the edge into the deep abyss below. He couldn't get his sister, Mike and now Aerial out of his mind believing they had all gone over that cliff and not knowing whether any of them were dead or alive.

At that very moment he could feel his body starting to freeze up. He wasn't sure what was happening to him, but he knew it was probably the same old thing that always seemed to happen to him whenever he was in a tough situation and once again it caused him not to think clearly.

Then his eyes closed. He didn't consciously close them. They just closed and at that moment in time he was wishing he had never come to this place and he had never met Aerial and he had never gone with his friends that night to the crazy old man's house.

But just as it seemed to him that all hope was lost, another thought came over him. Maybe I shouldn't be wishing for anything at this moment in time, he thought. Maybe there is something more important I should be doing right now. He recalled again what his father had told him about the story with the family Plymouth.

"You will only have one chance to do what is right, right now."

And just then a calmness came over him that wasn't like any feeling he had ever felt before.

Chapter Twenty – A design limitation

"This is strange," mumbled Maynard.

He adjusted the electric lamp on his mahogany desk. Then he peered deeply into his computer screen. Grey circles sagged beneath his almost closed eyes on his peaked drawn face. On the far side of the dimly lit room a lifeless body lay crumpled on the cold hard floor.

Her eyelids fluttered twice, then opened.

"Where am I?"

She reached up blocking the bright light from the right side of her face. She tilted her head and squinted. She recalled the violent wind, then the falling. Her neck lurched back. Disconnected images flashed through her head. A single thought struck her brain. I must be– dead.

"Lindsey? Are you ok?" She felt relieved to hear a familiar voice.

She blinked. Then blinked again. She had known him all his life, but something was wrong. All wrong. She recalled the summer of the Lion King play. Over and over they practiced until it was right. The neighbors came and watched. They smiled. And then it was all over. Just like that it was over. She recalled walking into her house and up the creaking stairs to her room in the back. She had grown that day and was proud of what they had all done, but at the same time she felt a sadness that it was over.

"Where the devil are we?

"I haven't a clue," replied Mike. "But we aren't alone." He pointed across the room at a prematurely greying man. He was working diligently at his mahogany desk. He wore brown sandals with no socks, cutoff jeans and a plaid short sleeve shirt. There was a redish dime-sized rash on the inside of his right wrist, and a brown lesion just above his left ankle. She rubbed her chin.

"We'll need to keep an eye on him."

She read the name Maynard Jackson printed on his laminated badge. Beyond Maynard was a thick steel door leading to a brightly lit hallway. She looked at Mike.

"We need to do a little investigating."

She stepped into the hall and then looked back over her shoulder. The words, Room 205– Dedicated to Project 2010, were printed in bold green letters above the door.

She peered down the massive hallway. It gave her an eerie feeling as if she had been here before, but she couldn't remember when. She sensed it had something to do with her father.

Thinking of her father and this place reminded her of a park near her home where her father would push her on the swings when she was young and where they would watch the other children play. Many of the other children who went to that park lived high up on a hill on the far side of the park in the big red brick building.

Her brother had a friend who lived there too. They called it Saint Ann's Orphanage and it was where the kids who didn't have parents lived. Pat's friend had told him about the nuns and the twenty-five toilets all in a row without any stalls. Pat knew there were exactly twenty-five. He had counted them when he went inside one day with his friend.

"I wasn't expecting to see you today, Lindsey."

She jerked her head startled by the stranger's voice. He was staring at her and it made her feel awkward. She thought that she knew him, but when she tried to remember, she couldn't. She decided to just play along pretending she knew him.

"Hello. We're on a school project. This is my classmate Michael," she calmly replied.

The man's eyes scanned the boy from head to toe. She glanced again down the long hallway. The orphans from St. Ann's were still on her mind. Whenever she thought of them a feeling came over her as if something was missing in her life, but she could never quite pinpoint where that feeling was coming from. For some unexplainable reason it felt to her like she had some connection to orphans, but she didn't know why.

"Seems a bit young to be in your class, Lindsey." He said it using a curious tone as he continued to size up the boy.

"Mike is very smart. Don't be fooled by his height."

He looked at Mike again.

"On what side of town do you live young man?"

"The West Side," replied Mike. "I live right down the street from Lindsey."

"I'll bet you play ball in her backyard too." She looked at him again. He knows about our house, she thought to herself.

"I haven't seen your mother in a few years. How is she doing?"

"She's been thinking about going back to work now that Pat and myself are older."

Back in room 205 Maynard slowly lowered his right elbow down on the arm of his chair. Then he plopped his chin into the palm of his right hand.

"This is going to be tougher than I thought," he mused.

He slid back getting himself into a more comfortable position. Gently, he stroked his grey beard. Suddenly, his head popped back up, as he leaned forward.

"Looks like a design limitation– too many objects in the game," he uttered.

He stroked his beard again. Then he double-clicked the snake.

Chapter Twenty-One – A gate

"Facts Fred. Just stick to the facts."

Fred gulped. He admired Vice-President Washburn. He admired his ability to think fast, especially under fire. Thinking fast wasn't one of Fred's strong points. Given time, Fred liked thinking through all the issues. But this was different and he hated even thinking about it right now because he had too many other things on his mind.

They marched down the corridor heading for the Executive conference room. It was all up to Fred. He held his pointer in his shaking left hand. He was playing with it pulling the tip out, then pushing it back in. It was a nervous habit of his.

He didn't have a clue what he was going to say which isn't good for Fred who likes to be completely prepared for situations like this. But, in this case, he just didn't have time to prepare and think ahead about how to best handle this situation.

He tried to think fast. And as he did his forehead started to sweat. He could see the door just up ahead and he wished he could just use it and get the hell out of there. Random thoughts slipped in and out of his mind. No one was supposed to get hurt. Images of his children passed before him. His stomach felt like it was turning inside out.

Why do these things always happen to me? he thought to himself.

Then he reached to wipe his head. It felt like fire and as fast as he wiped the sweat away more beads of sweat appeared.

The customer entered the room. It was quiet at first, but the quiet didn't help. In fact, it just made it worse. His mind was somewhere else, and he needed all of the powers of his mind to be focused now if he was to work his way out of this mess.

Think man think, Fred thought to himself, but his brain wasn't listening. The door closed. Fred stared at the wall. It was blank, just like his mind.

A scraping sound of shoes shuffling toward the front of the room was the only sound heard. Fred didn't know the sound was coming from his own shoes. Fred's head was tilted down. His body was bent. He turned peering back at the stern faces. His eyes met the Vice-President's. He stopped cold. Then he raised his chin and smiled.

"Ladies and gentlemen, I'm going to tell you an honest story. In fact, it is a story you will find hard to believe, but it is absolutely the god's honest truth and up until now it has been a very well-kept secret."

His smile widened and his chin popped up a notch. Fred was feeling more confident now because he knew what he had accomplished and he was so proud of it that he had wanted to share it with the world for the longest time and now was his chance.

"We found a gate." The words just slipped out. Then he grinned from ear to ear.

"And you'll never guess what we've been able to connect to on the other side."

General Switzer nudged Jack Washburn.

"Is he joking with us?"

The blood drained from the Vice-President's face. He called for a five minute break.

"Fred, have you gone crazy! Think about what you're saying! Facts Fred! Get back to the facts!" Fred nodded to the Vice-President.

Then he scurried down the hall and into room 205.

"Meg, I need the latest status immediately!" She pointed across the room. Maynard's eyes were glued to his screen and his fingers were moving at incredible speed.

"He's been going all night. We don't know how to stop him."

Fred looked over and saw Maynard. He seemed to be typing at about five times the speed that was possible for human beings. But then again, this didn't surprise Fred because he knew Maynard wasn't exactly human.

Meg glanced at her watch, then reached for her coat.

"I have a meeting with Jesse's teacher in half an hour."

"Meg, you can't leave now! We're almost out of time."

She jerked open the side drawer of her desk pulling out her purse.

"Meg, I need hard facts!" She slammed the drawer shut and started toward the door.

"You want hard facts!" She opened the door.

"The hard fact is Jesse's almost out of time too!"

The door slammed behind her. Fred turned and looked across the room.

"Maynard!" he yelled as he moved toward him.

Maynard's eyes were still glued to his screen and his fingers were now moving four times faster than they were just moments before.

"Maynard Jackson!" Fred yelled again.

He was still moving toward him. Fred reached out and grabbed him giving him a good shake. Fred only wanted to get his attention. He only wanted to find out what Maynard knew. But when he shook him it did something to Maynard and his fingers began to move even faster. And then even faster. Up and down his keyboard they raced. And his eyes were acting funny too– rolling up and then down inside his head.

Fred pulled both his hands away quickly.

"Oh no! Look what I've done now!" he said to himself as he stumbled backwards into the hall.

Then he turned and ran down the hall. He stopped at the door to the conference room to catch his breath. He wanted the customer to think he had everything under control. Casually he strolled to the front of the room.

"Ladies and gentlemen. I have a hard fact to share with you."

All eyes were fixed on Fred.

"We've had a complication."

Then he hesitated.

"We need more time to get the last bug out." The room fell silent, but only for an instant.

"You've blown billions and now you want more to get the last bug out!" blurted out General Switzer.

He stood up. Then he leaned over and raising his hand to his mouth he whispered in Vice-President Washburn's ear.

"You can expect a stop work order within twenty-four hours!"

Then he marched out. The others followed.

Fred stood in the front of the room, now all alone. His pointer was still in his hand. He gently laid it down beside the projector. There were no beads of sweat on his forehead now. His stomach wasn't churning anymore. He walked to the back of the room. Then turned and looked once more.

Fred was fifty-three years old. He flicked the light switch off and shut the door and then he walked back to his office for what would be the last time.

Chapter Twenty-Two – A fierce hunter

Pat gazed upward. The bluish-green tint in the sky seemed to calm his nerves. He drew a breath holding it in for a second before letting it out. Then he peered over the edge.

"Aerial!" he screeched.

Aerial was alive! But he was in deep trouble.

It shocked the boy seeing his friend that way. The collar of Aerial's shirt had caught on a jagged rock just a few feet down over the edge of the cliff. Aerial was hanging literally by a thread.

Instantly Pat dropped to his knees putting his own safety out of his mind. He reached over the edge with his right arm stretched as far as it could go. He looked down. He felt woozy, so he closed his eyes. He imagined his arm, wrist and fingers all working together as if they were one. He stretched again. His body began to shake.

Keeping his eyes shut he stretched yet again. The shaking worsened. Pat thought his body was coming apart, but he blocked the thought from his mind and stretched even more. His hand reached the collar of Aerial's shirt. He clutched hold of it.

He had used his last ounce of strength, but he refused to let his mind know it as he pulled Aerial to safety. Completely exhausted, they laid along the edge of the cliff. Pat peered upward. A puzzled look crossed his face.

"I touched you?" Aerial just nodded.

"We don't completely understand it."

Aerial stood up. He brushed the dirt and grime off his pants. He straightened the sleeves of his shirt. Pat noticed something behind him. It was high up in the sky and moving fast.

Suddenly, it turned and swooped downward. There was no time for explanation. Pat lunged knocking Aerial to the ground just out of the path of the sleek bird's outstretched claws.

"It's not safe here," gasped Aerial. "Follow me." He said it quickly, then rushed for cover in the rocks.

"What was that?" asked Pat.

"They're called Cormorants," replied Aerial. The boy peered up. The bird with its bright yellow and deep red feathers sat perfectly still on a rocky ledge above.

"Do you have Cormorants near the cliffs in Farthington?" asked Aerial.

"No, but we have pidgeons near the Courthouse," replied Pat.

"It's not the same," said Aerial.

"The Cormorant is a fierce hunter. It uses its deep pouch to keep its catch. They're nice to look at, but never let your guard down around one. They never sleep. And once they get a thought in their head, they never give up. Never."

Aerial drew a slow breath.

"They say Eagles have good eyes, but the Cormorant's are better. They can spot a six inch fish a foot under water from a mile away."

Aerial hesitated.

"But they're not born that way."

Pat turned and looked at Aerial.

"Growing up is hard for them too," said Aerial. He looked right at Pat.

"The mother is critical. She teaches them everything." Aerial looked down.

"It's a mystery how they survive."

"The young are hatched blind, and downright ugly. They're covered with an inky black goo. The mother protects its young and patiently teaches it to survive. She never leaves her young alone– until it's time. Somehow, she knows. She doesn't give it a test. She just knows. One day she swoops down for some food, only this time she doesn't come back. She never comes back."

The story of the Cormorant reminded Pat of the first time he went fishing. Six hours and only a few lousy bites on his worm. He recalled the feeling he had that day. For six long hours he had tried and tried. He only wanted to catch one, not to keep it. Just to see how it felt. And to get the pin for his scout uniform. By early afternoon he had begun to pick up the knack of casting. He had even learned the importance of keeping quiet– something that didn't come natural to the boy.

But by late in the day it had all become too much. Pat was losing his patience and his mother, who had agreed to go with him because she was helping out as one of the scout leaders, had long since lost hers.

It was the usual consequence. Grounded. Why does mom always do that to me, he wondered all the way home. Why does she always take my friends away? He looked up at the Cormorant. He thought again of Aerial's words.

"Only this time she doesn't come back."

"Quick, we must head for the mountains," said Aerial.

"It won't give up."

In room 205 a message was blinking on Maynard's screen. He tried to focus his eyes, but he was having difficulty. He raised his left hand and slapped himself once on the side of his head. It seemed to momentarily stabilize his eyes. Slowly he read the message: "System Error–Unable to complete request."

"Must be a bad spot on the disk," he mused.

"I'd better reformat. And if that doesn't work, I'll just chuck the whole thing and start over."

He clicked the snake. The message read:

"Are you sure? All data will be DESTROYED."

Maynard clicked again.

Chapter Twenty-Three – Go fast, take chances

At sixteen years old Patrick McMichaels spent little time standing still. His life was full of movement. Most things that weren't moving fast Pat found boring. But the Cormorant was different. The Cormorant moved fast, but also stood still.

They had returned to the mountains. Pat was standing still watching a Cormorant sitting quietly perched on a branch in a tree. It was the first time in the boy's life he had actually stood still for any length of time watching something that wasn't moving faster than himself.

He had been to the mountains before. When he was young he had come with his parents and sister, but he didn't remember much from that time other than feeling bored. He was feeling something different now. He gazed at the trees. Motionless trees. Trees that seemed to move only at the will of the wind.

He was trying to keep his mind occupied. But all he could find to occupy it were the trees– the massive motionless boring trees. Movement meant life to the boy. He knew that trees lived, but it was a different kind of life to the boy– not what he called living. He knew he had always functioned better in motion. It helped him think. He didn't know why, he just knew it did.

He recalled again Mike's father, Roger, when guiding Mike in his skiing.

"Go fast, take chances."

He had always liked recalling those words. They helped his best friend become a world class skier, but they also helped Pat in ways he could not fully describe.

He had read about the giant Sequoias out west. They lived thousands of years, but the thought of life with limited movement as trees troubled him. He looked up. A giant tree stood close by. He looked at its sprawling branches. Up, up and away they went. Seemingly to nowhere, just up.

At times he felt like the tree. He felt he was going nowhere. He wondered how the tree felt about where it was going. Did it want to move in other directions and faster? Did the tree dream of moving late at night when no one watched? Did it dream of dancing its way through the forest with only the moonlight to see?

He reached out touching the bark. He knew the bark protected the tree, but what did a tree need protection from? Who was going to hurt a tree? He moved his fingers up and down sensing the trees inner strength. It was a different kind of strength from what he had observed with his sister's recent heroics. He didn't completely understand that kind of strength, but he felt it just the same.

His thoughts were suddenly interrupted by a buzzing sound. He could feel the vibration coming through his feet. He looked down, then back up. A throng of Virlingreal specialized Components were marching their way across a distant hill. Steel blades from razor sharp buzz saws they were holding glistened in the sun. Trees fell. Trees that had lived thousands of years. Trees that had never hurt another. Trees that never had a chance to dance in the moonlight.

It made no sense to the boy. None of it made any sense and he so badly wanted it all to make sense.

Is this what war is like? the boy wondered.

Is this what his father had tried to tell him about the real world? He desperately wanted to understand and he wanted everything to make sense. He wanted to know the answer, but at the same time he didn't.

When he was younger Fred had told him there was a right time to die and that death was not something to fear because it's not the end. It's just a new beginning. He had no clue what his father was trying to tell him when he told him that, just like a lot of other stuff his father told him that never made any sense.

Fred told his son about a talk Steve Jobs, the creator of Apple and Pixar gave at a commencement address to Stanford University. Steve started out the address by telling the graduates that this was as close as he ever got to graduating from college.

Steve had dropped out in his freshman year. But then he hung around attending classes that interested him, rather than the ones that he had to take when he was trying to get a degree.

In that speech Steve talked about the power of death, and referred to it as the greatest invention of man because it forces one to realize time is limited in life. It gives you a needed sense of urgency in life, Steve said. He also said he never would have created the amazing things he invented if it weren't for his awareness of his own impending death.

Knowing you are going to die gives you something else, Pat's father had told him. It gives you the freedom to really live and be completely aware of your life. Too many people go through life feeling like they are living on egg shells, his father had told him.

When Pat was young and losing himself between the racks of clothes at the department store where his parents shopped, his sister had told him he was adopted. She made it up just to scare him, but on that day when his sister told him that, Pat thought a part of him had died. It was the first time he thought he might know what death feels like.

"We must leave immediately," said Aerial. The boy looked up.

"I want to come back."

"You can always come back," replied Aerial,

"but it won't be the same. It will never be the same again."

The words echoed through Pat's brain. And those old feelings that always seemed to come back inside him came back once again.

Only this time he didn't feel like running like he had always felt before when those feelings came over him– those feelings that made him want to run, and keep running as fast as he could all the way home and crawl under his bed.

This time he was ready to stand still and stay calm like the Cormorant and the trees and face up to who he was and what he had done. This time he was ready because he knew it was his only chance to do the right thing at this moment in his life.

Chapter Twenty-Four –
Stay cool, think straight

"Would you like some help?"

She jerked her head up surprised to hear the man's voice again. She didn't trust him, but she didn't know why.

"We'd love some help."

Something from a long time ago she had forgotten, or unconsciously blanked from her mind, flashed through her head. It was an image of a dark green car pulling up in front of her home.

"Sir?" The man glanced over his shoulder.

"Were you talking to me?" He squinted at the boy.

"Yes, sir. I was wondering what you do here?"

Lindsey's eyes were glued to the man. It was starting to come back to her, but a part of her was fighting to forget. She was nine at the time. He wore a grey suit and a red tie and she watched him through the front window of her home on Cherry Street as he got out of his car and walked toward the house. Her mother opened the door.

"We teach our employees and young adults how to handle the difficult situations they face in life."

"Difficult situations?" You mean like getting a fire started when you don't have matches?" The man chuckled.

"This isn't the boy scouts."

He was younger then, but there was no mistake about it. It was the same man. Her mother politely asked him to sit and make himself comfortable. Then she brought him a drink. Her brother was squirming on the floor, fidgeting like he often did when he was young.

She was staring at the man now and realized that she had better stop or he would get suspicious. She glanced down the hallway, wondering again, where they could be.

This man had come to their house. She was certain of it. And now they were in this new strange place where someone knew her.

"Well, what can you teach me about handling difficult situations?"

The man cleared his throat, then drew back his chin.

"We can teach you to stay cool and think straight when your forehead is beading up with sweat and your throat goes dry and your inside turns inside out and you got that feeling."

The man poked Mike once in the belly. Then he snickered.

"You know that feeling?" Then he poked the boy again, only this time harder.

"Yes sir. I got it now." The man chuckled again.

He didn't chuckle that night, thought Lindsey. She recalled their voices getting louder. She didn't understand the words, but she knew they were upsetting her mother. Patrick was lying on his back staring at the ceiling. She recalled the man had a newspaper folded under his arm. He took it out and pointed to something in it. Then their voices got loud again. Casey, our dog, squealed, and Patrick was pulling his ear. The boy could never keep still.

"The way we teach our employees to stay cool and think straight is by first creating a stress-free workplace. Our employees are taught not to hold things inside. People don't think straight when they feel stressed. We even conduct lunch time seminars and encouraged everyone to participate. If they see anything that seems wrong we teach them to speak up. Our motto here is everyone's voice matters."

She didn't believe a word he was saying. It wasn't stress-free that night. How can he smile like that, she thought. Doesn't he think I remember. Maybe he thinks I was too young.

She recalled how her father talked to her that night. He was acting like it wasn't a big deal. Like it was just another day.

"Your mother will need to rely on you while I'm gone," her father had told her.

"Follow me. I'll show you how stress-free it is in our workplace." They passed room 205 as they moved down the hall.

"Can we see what goes on in here?" asked Lindsey. He shook his head.

"In this room our engineers are working on a special project and they are on the brink of a major breakthrough. We're finding–" He stopped in the middle of his sentence.

"I'd better not say anymore," he mumbled to himself.

His words triggered another memory in the girl's head. They talked about breakthroughs that night. And it was breakthroughs she heard her father talk about in his sleep. She was now seeing more pieces to this puzzle, but still struggling to make them fit.

"Lindsey, I have to conduct an interview with a young candidate we are thinking about hiring here at the Lab." She looked up.

"I hope I've helped you."

The man smiled and then walked down the hall. He said he had to make a phone call that night, she recalled. Then he walked into the other room and her father began to talk to her about what it would be like when he was gone.

As they moved down the hall she was jolted back from her memories as she overheard a conversation by a couple of employees.

"Did you hear about Fred McMichaels?"

"Hear what?"

"The authorities want to question him about using funds from his project illegally. And it wasn't the first time. I heard he got caught for the same problem a long time ago and had to spend time in prison."

"Yes, now I remember it all," thought Lindsey.

She recalled the doorbell rang again. Two more men in suits walked in. They opened their wallets and flashed their badges. They told her father not to pack and that he wouldn't be able to take any of his things. She recalled how tense life had become while her father was gone. How they kept it from her brother.

Then suddenly, she just stopped. Mike heard it too. More people were talking in the hall. They were talking about billions of dollars being spent illegally and about a failed secret project.

She turned and pressed her back against the hallway wall. Slowly she inched her way downward toward the floor. She shook her head. Her chin drooped between her knees. She didn't want to think about this anymore. Her face grew red. Her torso stiff. She turned face down against the floor. She tightened her fist raising it above the ground and then began to pound it down again and again on the cold hard floor.

Over and over she pounded. Her eyes were shut tight. Mike tried to stop her, but she easily pushed him away. Then, suddenly, she just stopped.

She looked down at the blood dripping from her knuckles onto the floor. Then she looked up. It was Mike. But it wasn't Mike. Just like it had been her father that night, but it wasn't her father. It couldn't have been her father.

Just then she heard another familiar voice. She took a deep breath. Slowly she stood steadying herself against the hallway wall. She pulled a blue neckerchief from her pocket wrapping it around her bruised hand.

She heard the voice again. It was the voice of her father. She turned and looked at Mike.

"We must be inside the Jefferson Lab. Let's just stay close and keep out of sight so we can figure out what the heck is going on here."

Chapter Twenty-Five – A serious game

She didn't want her father to know he was being followed. Fred opened the door leading outside the secured facility. He was planning to go directly home and go out for a long run to help him forget this disastrous day. A man he didn't know was standing near his car.

"Is your name Fred McMichaels?" Fred nodded.

"Can you tell us what's going on inside?" Fred squinted.

"Got nothing to hide. Inside we're opening up young people's minds."

"Where did your staff do their residency?" Fred shook his head.

"We don't use medical people, if that's what you're poking at. We use biologists, chemists and software engineering professionals."

"You mean to say you're operating on young people without medical trained doctors?"

"You don't understand. We have all the expertise we need. And we have developed the most advanced hybrid gaming-learning environment ever devised."

The man looked down at his notebook, then back up at Fred.

"Mr. McMichaels, are you saying that the Jefferson Lab has spent billions of taxpayer dollars– and it's all just a game?"

Fred's eyes bulged from his head.

"Of course not! It's real, but not really. You see it's a serious game."

Fred scrunched his nose.

"And what about your missing children and the neighborhood boy?"

"What do you know about it!" snapped Fred.

"Have you been opening up their minds too?"

The man peered at Fred out the side of his right eye.

"Mr. McMichaels what about this five year gap in your resume? We understand you served time in prison. Was that for illegal use of government funds too?"

Fred started to mumble. His mind began to wander. Then he took a deep breath, and tried to gathered his thoughts.

"No. absolutely not. My prison time had nothing to do with my work at the Jefferson Lab. It was just because of a little mistake I made a long time ago using CRISPR technology to modify my daughter's DNA."

Lindsey's eyes bulged from her head, and her jaw dropped almost to the ground. She heard the words, but her mind refused to process them. She turned seemingly dazed by what she heard, and slowly walked back inside the lab and down the long hall leading back to room 205.

Maynard was staring at his screen. Lindsey, still dazed, tried to get her mind to think about something else—anything else. She stared at Maynard. What keeps him going, she wondered. He doesn't even know the project has been cancelled.

"Maynard!" she screamed.

He looked up. His eyes were red and glassy.

"It's over Maynard. The project's been cancelled. Go home! You look terrible!"

He squinted. Then he mumbled something incoherent at his screen.

"He's confused," said Mike. She looked at Mike.

"That's an understatement."

She ran to Maynard reaching out grabbing and shaking him firmly.

"Maynard!" she screamed again.

"Why are you still working so hard. Do you have any idea what my father did?"

Maynard turned and looked at the girl. He shook his head and his eyes cleared as something the girl said seemed to bring him to his senses.

"Yes Lindsey. I know exactly what your father did. He was just trying to do everything he could to make all of our dreams—yours, mine, your brother's and Mike's– come true."

"But he tried to change me into someone other than who I am."

Maynard nodded.

"He knew he made a mistake on that one, but he did everything he could to fix it."

A puzzled look came over Lindsey.

"What do you mean Maynard?"

"Oh nothing," replied Maynard nonchalantly.

"No. You have to tell me Maynard. You said he did everything he could to fix it. What else did he do to me?"

"No. No. You don't understand. He didn't do anything else to you. He finally understood that parents can only do so much for their kids and when they try too hard to fix them it just doesn't work. He finally understood that in spades!"

"Maynard. Don't you think I deserve to know what my father did to fix a mistake that affected my life big time?"

Maynard at first said nothing, but then slowly replied to the girl.

"Your father is a good man. If it wasn't for him I wouldn't be half the man I am today. But that's another story and I don't think we should get into it right now."

"What are you saying Maynard? Did he modify your DNA too? Did he try to turn you into someone other than you?"

"Lindsey, calm down. I don't want to get into it. It's a complicated story. And anyway I like the way I turned out. "

But Lindsey was not about to calm down.

"Complicated story you say! Don't you understand we are talking about people's lives. You can't just go around changing someone's DNA willy-nilly. Doesn't he know the consequences? Of all people, my father should certainly understand that. "

"He does Lindsey. He completely understands the seriousness of everything we are doing here at the lab."

She shook her head angrily.

"Ok. I see that you are not about to calm down. I didn't want to do this, but I see no other choice. I think there is someone else you need to talk to."

Then Maynard picked up the phone and started dialing.

"Erin, could you stop over to room 205. There is someone here I think you should meet."

Chapter Twenty-Six – Crazy guidance

"Pat, it's time."

"What do you mean?" questioned the boy.

"I mean we can't keep running like this." Aerial drew a breath. A puzzled look crossed Pat's face.

"Where will we go?"

"I have a plan. We're going through the window." Pat's face paled.

"It's not what you think," responded Aerial quickly.

Then he raised his right index finger.

"First, I'm going to teach you the art of climbing." Aerial hesitated.

"And I'm not talking about trees in your backyard. You're going to learn to scale cliffs that go straight up hundreds of feet."

Pat stared at him. He didn't know what to think. He wondered if Aerial's brain had started spinning again. But this time his eyes looked clear and stable.

"We'll start in the morning. Now get some rest."

Early the next morning Aerial began to teach the boy the fundamentals of ropes, pulleys, and climbing. He showed Pat a rack containing a series of metal bars. Then he demonstrated how to use the system to control speed. Aerial made it look easy, but when Pat tried he couldn't get his left hand out of the way of his right. The system felt strange to the boy and it worried him.

"With time you'll get the hang of it," said Aerial.

He handed the system to the boy.

"Put it in your hands. Work it up and down, over and over. Do it until you can do it in your sleep without thinking. It's got to feel like breathing."

Aerial hesitated.

"You can't be depending on your mind all the time. When we go for real, your mind will be busy with other things."

Pat spent hours and hours practicing guided by Aerial's watchful eye. Over and over he worked with the system. Up and down he moved the bars, again and again. At first he did it slowly concentrating on technique. Then gradually he did it more quickly and with less thought. After each practice session the boy found himself more and more exhausted. He wanted to rest. Just to take a little time for a walk in the woods to let his mind rest. But Aerial said no. He kept driving the boy. He kept telling him to keep his mind focused and that there would be plenty of time to rest later.

"Going down is an art. It requires skill, muscle and thought. But don't be fooled. This is no game of brute strength."

Aerial glanced at his right arm.

"We'll be going down into that same pit that claimed your sister and friend."

He looked up at Pat.

"You won't be able to forget it. But you'll need to put it out of your mind."

He stretched his right arm out and winced. Pat stared at him concerned that Aerial was in pain.

"Not to worry. Just an old nagging war injury. Nineteen hundred feet, straight down," said Aerial. Then he hesitated.

"When we go for real it will all be planned, including what to do if the plan fails." He hesitated again.

"And no matter how many times you do it in your mind, when we go for real it's going to be different." Aerial drew a breath.

"It's always different when you do it for real." Pat's eyes were looking down.

"One last thing." The boy looked up at Aerial. He was holding onto his right arm again.

"Once we start on this trip, we can't start over. This time it's going to be for real." His face looked cold and weathered.

"Do you think you're ready?" The boy didn't answer. He didn't need to, but Aerial knew what was going on inside him.

"It won't go away," said Aerial. "You just need to live with it. Now get some sleep. We go tonight."

Pat closed his eyes, but his mind refused to let go. He had been to the edge. Just to look down– to get the feel. Each time he imagined what it would be like. Each time he told himself he could do it. He had practiced over and over, for hours and hours, until he didn't even need to think. Tonight, he thought, will be no different. I've done this a thousand times. I could do it in my sleep. He said it aloud.

"Tonight will be no different."

But as the time drew near he knew it wasn't true. As hard as he tried to pretend that everything would be the same, that he would just walk to the edge and nothing would be different, deep down inside he knew it wasn't true. It would never be the same. Never could be the same again.

And at that moment what he couldn't get out of his mind the most were all the things that just didn't make sense to him. Things his father had tried to explain.

One minute Fred was pushing the boy telling him he needed to be focused and have a clear goal in life. And the next minute he was telling him not to worry. Telling him he had all the time in the world. Telling him its ok to make mistakes.

How is a kid to have a clue how to live with crazy guidance like that, he wondered.

He recalled some other words that his father kept posted on the door to his office from an old-time baseball player named Satchel Page, who Pat had never heard of. More words, just words, that never made sense to him–

"Work like you don't need the money, love like you've never been hurt, dance like nobody is watching."

What in the world did those words mean? The boy was thinking back now to something Aerial had told him just before he went to sleep that night.

"The lesson I want you to learn isn't how to get great at ropes and pulleys, or strengthening your muscles to the point where you can perform great feats, but rather learning how to help yourself by forgetting yourself and helping someone else along the way."

Aerial was starting to sound like his father, thought the boy, with his seemingly coded messages that played with the boy's mind.

When Aerial said those words, it reminded the boy once again of the story his father had told him about the day Fred's father picked up the drunk in the family Plymouth.

Fred had talked to the boy about life that day and he told his son,

"We just don't know when those moments will happen in our lives, so we need to be ready whenever the time comes."

It was time now. It was one of those moments and the boy knew it as he stood on the edge looking down. Down, down, down. And thinking. Just thinking. On the outside the boy was a picture of concentration. On the inside his insides were pulling him apart. There would be no turning back. No starting over. He wasn't even concerned about that now. He had made his decision. But then Aerial had to go and start in again. Why now? the boy wondered. Why would he do it now just when I need to keep my concentration? And the memories flooded back.

Aerial stared at him.

"They never caught the boys."

And Pat knew it was true. And he wanted to crawl back under his bed just like that night four years ago. But then he thought again.

Why should I be scared now? Why now? It could've changed my life, but it didn't. He had thought at the time they'd send him away– probably to a reform school upstate. That's where he'd meet the hard-core types. He'd read about what happens to good kids who go bad. They get sent upstate. And that would change him– really change him. Upstate he'd learn more– lots more– like how to pull a real job. Not just kid's stuff. And by the time he'd get back his friends wouldn't even know him. Of course, he'd still have the same parts. But that would be on the inside. On the outside no one would know. It would be like he was someone else and only Pat would know. It would be his secret. And in a strange way he actually felt relieved to think he was going to become someone else. He looked up and shook his head.

"But I'm sixteen now," he said to himself.

"And it never happened that way."

Why should I be worried now, he thought. Even if they did know– even if Aerial knew– what could they do to me now?

He knew he had left a trail of blood. But no one had done anything about it. He was certain of it. He had followed the stories in the newspapers carefully. They gathered no blood samples. There was no DNA testing. He doubted they had any real proof at all. He snickered to himself.

"If anyone brings it up, I'll just deny everything. I'll just act cool."

It started when he was nine. That's when Mike first told him about the crazy old man who lived three streets over. Mike said the man never mowed his lawn and that he only put his garbage out late at night. And just once a year. And he said the man never went outside– never. Except to his car, but not to drive it. He kept everything he owned in the trunk. His house wasn't far from the park. It was high up on a dark hill. It was set back away from the street on the opposite side from Saint Ann's Orphanage.

They had planned that night for months—Just Pat and Mike. Planned it just like the tunnel, only this job was different.

Everything had to be right. And when the time came Pat McMichaels wasn't one bit afraid. It might have been better if he was. It was one of those hot and sticky August nights in Farthington. It was the night they would learn the truth. No more guesswork.

If he wasn't crazy– if they were just made up stories– then they'd at least know the truth. No one ever is hurt by the truth.

Except that night. That night Pat just wasn't thinking when he picked up the rock and let fly. Threw it straighter than he ever threw before. Then it all got crazy. Like a dream. Like one of those terrible dreams that turn into a nightmare and you wake up sweating and your heart pounding. But this wasn't a nightmare. Nightmares end. Nightmares go away.

He came from nowhere, recalled Pat. And with those eyes and head and making that noise. He didn't even sound human. Pat could hear the noise again in his head as he thought back to that night. That night that seemed to never go away.

The old crazy man just kept coming. Pat's heart was pounding then, and it was pounding again now, like it always did, whenever he thought about it. The next thing he remembered was running as fast as he could go down Semetary Place through the park heading toward the river with the old man right on his heels. And he kept saying those same words.

"Bad boys. Bad boys."

I don't know how many times he said it, Pat thought to himself. But those words stuck in his brain.

The next day he couldn't stop shaking.

"Stay away from the crazy old man," the neighborhood kids used to say. "He's different."

Pat said his name aloud. Jay Wilson. Then he said it again, only this time he said it louder.

JAY WILSON, as if by saying it loud enough he could somehow make it all different.

"Secure the pulleys. Drop the ropes." Aerial was still staring at the boy and at that moment looking deep into Aerial's eyes he suddenly realized who Aerial really was.

Chapter Twenty-Seven – A theory

Erin had just arrived at room 205.

"Erin, this is Lindsey McMichaels. She is Fred McMichael's daughter. I think you know Fred."

A small smile crossed the corner of Maynard's face as he said it.

Erin just nodded.

"I think the two of you will have a very interesting conversation and I'd love to stick around for it, but I have another crisis to attend to."

And with that introduction Maynard walked out the door.

From the moment Erin entered the room a strange feeling came over Lindsey. It was the kind of feeling you get when you meet someone and you think you already know them, but you can't remember where you know them from.

As an example, before Erin said one word, Lindsey somehow felt she knew exactly what the young girl's voice would sound like, but she had no idea why she knew it.

No one should be surprised by this type of situation because it is not at all unusual for people to experience these kinds of things. Her father, Fred, once had a very similar experience upon meeting a woman at a get together at one of his cousin's homes. He knew exactly what the woman's voice would sound like and he told her he felt like he saw her and spoke with her every day of his life.

Even more oddly, the woman told Fred she felt the same way, and they both laughed about it, agreeing that sometime in the next few days they would surely run into each other and then they would realize why they knew each other so well. But, even more strangely, they never saw each other again. At least, in this life.

"Hi Lindsey. It's nice to meet you. You are amazingly tall. When I was younger I dreamed of being tall, but it just wasn't to be."

"Erin, I had the strangest feeling when you walked into the room like I have known you all my life, but I just can't for the life of me remember where I know you from."

"That's interesting, because I had the same feeling. My parents told me I was adopted and they said I might have a sister and a brother, but they couldn't give me any details. Could you tell me a little bit about yourself and then maybe we can figure this mystery out?"

"Sure. I'm nineteen years old. I grew up just a few miles from here in Farthington on Cherry Street and I attend Farthington University where I play on the basketball team. I am a sophomore and I am hoping to one day play professional basketball. I have devoted my entire life to basketball and it is my dream to become a professional and to be the very best at what I do. In fact, I usually practice from sun up to sun down except for the last few days which have been rather hectic in my life. But I don't think I need to go into all that right now."

"Ok. What you say fits. I am ten years old and my mother said that she thought my older sister was nine years older. So, I think there is a good chance you are my sister."

"But Erin, why in the world would my parents give you up? I could see my idiot father coming up with some crazy idea to get rid of you, but I don't think my mother would have let him get away with it if she had anything to say about it."

"I think you are right, but maybe that is just it. Maybe she didn't have anything to say about it. Maybe she didn't even know I was born and being raised across town. By the way I don't live far from you. I was brought up just a few miles from Cherry Street on Bennett Avenue."

"How in the world could my mother possibly not know she had another daughter?"

"I have a theory, and they say I am rather smart for my age. I have already graduated from high school and I am now attending the Boston Conservatory of Music."

"That's incredible. Please tell me your theory. I'm all ears!"

"Well, I think your father wanted you to be a great basketball player just like you wanted it. Right?"

"Yes. He was very involved in my early basketball development years. So tell me more about your theory. "

"Well, since I have been working out here at the Jefferson Lab as a part time employee I have been learning quite a bit about what they do here related to research with the CRISPR technology. Do you know about CRISPR?"

"I've heard of it. I know they use it to modify a person's DNA. In fact, I just found out that my father modified my DNA and that he actually went to prison for a few years because what he did to me was illegal."

"You got it. Now let me ask you something. Did your father ever regret that decision and maybe try to do something to fix his mistake?"

"Yes. I think you're on to something. Maynard had just said something to me about my father knowing he made a mistake and trying to fix it."

She stopped and looked at Erin.

"Maybe you aren't just my sister."

Erin nodded.

"I am thinking the same thing you are."

"Do you think our father could have used my DNA to clone you?"

"I know they understand the cloning process here at the lab and that is exactly my theory."

For the next few moments the girls just stared at each other. Then Erin broke the silence.

"We have a lot in common so I think this all makes sense. We both want to be the best we can be at whatever we are doing, and I even was a pretty good basketball player when I was young. But I decided to go into music because I was just too damn short! So I took up the flute instead."

Hearing all this, Lindsey was feeling overwhelmed and somewhat lost almost like what you might think people feel like when they have what is commonly referred to as an identity crisis.

"Erin, I love my life, but now I am wondering who I was supposed to be, and if I am living the wrong life."

"We all feel like we may be living the wrong life from time to time, even if no one messed with our DNA."

"Erin, you seem very wise for your young age."

"Thank you. Any wisdom I have is really due to you."

They both laughed.

"I have learned something else that might help you," continued Erin.

"I'm still all ears."

"Even though I want to become as good as I can be on my flute, and even though some of my teachers at the conservatory expect their students to practice from sun up to sun down, just like you are doing with basketball, I have found a better way that allows me to practice and get better without completely devoting my life to music."

"I'm still all ears."

Erin continued.

"I have found that I can practice my flute during the day when I don't even have my flute with me, and I find I have a little extra time. For example, I might be standing in line at the supermarket, and I have a few minutes, so I pretend I have my flute and I think about a hard sequence of notes I have been working on."

Erin then raised her fingers towards her lips as if playing an imaginary flute.

"I have found that by pretending to have my flute in my hands, my mind and my fingers start pretending too and together they work on the hard sequence. So, I don't really need to be practicing from sun up to sun down and this helps me get better without letting my musical goals get in the way of living my life."

"Funny you say that. My father once said something similar to me about not letting my goals get in the way of my life."

Chapter Twenty-Eight – Without thinking

Maynard was back at his workstation in room 205.

"Could Fred have actually done it?"

He chuckled as he said it to himself. Then he squinted at his computer screen. He was having difficulty focusing his eyes. He reached out and rotated the brightness knob as the phone rang on the far side of the room. He stood and tried to move toward it, but his legs weren't responding to his brain. He slammed into one wall, knocking over a garbage can, and then a file cabinet went crashing to the floor. Miraculously he reached the phone and lifted the receiver off the hook. He heard words, but the words were jumbled and made no sense to him.

Pat and Aerial were into their descent. Aerial looked down. He could see Maynard lying on the floor with the phone cord wrapped tightly around his neck.

"We must move quickly," said Aerial.

Downward and downward they scaled resetting anchors from one ledge to the next. Eight hundred feet. Nine hundred. One thousand. Suddenly, without any warning, everything just froze.

"Aerial, I'm caught."

Aerial said nothing. He seemed to be thinking. Then slowly he lifted his head looking over at Pat.

"What did you say?"

"It's my pulley. It's jammed." The boy was busy trying to free himself, but the more he struggled the tighter the knot became.

"It's no use. We'll need to activate the backup plan."

Once again, Aerial said nothing. He squinted.

"Aerial?"

Pat could see that Aerial's eyes were rolling again. What a time to have him fade out! thought Pat. He looked down. Someone was moving on the ground below. It was a girl. He looked closer. She was jumping up and down and waving with both her hands.

"Lindsey!" cried the boy.

"Lindsey! Lindsey!"

"Stop!" screamed Aerial. "Or you'll raise a Controller." Pat stopped instantly. Then he looked over at Aerial. His eyes were rolling again.

"Snap out of it, Aerial!"

Still Aerial didn't listen or he couldn't listen. Pat didn't know which, but he knew he had to do something. So, he took a deep breath and clenched his fist and let fly with a punishing left hook. Aerial's head snapped back. Then he heard a loud crack.

Motionless, Aerial dangled at the end of his rope.

Oh no, thought Pat, what have I done now?

He looked up. The sky was turning dark.

What's happening? Pat thought to himself.

Two Cormorants were circling.

He realized he may have made the situation far worse by striking Aerial. And he was starting to realize that nothing was going according to the plan, and even the backup plan wasn't working. But he realized this was no time to think about any of that.

So, he took a deep breath and told himself to keep calm. Then he told himself he knew what he was doing. He didn't believe a word of it, but he wasn't about to let that stop him now.

Then he thought to himself, if I could just get myself moving– if I could just find a way to get my body going faster, then I know I can figure out what I need to do next.

He looked around. He could see two walls, one in front and the other behind him. He leaned back pushing against one of the walls to help get his body moving. As his body started to move his left hand got close enough for him to grab hold of Aerial. Then he kicked with both his legs against the other wall and his body started to move faster and faster and as it did he was able to reach a ledge while still holding onto Aerial's lifeless body.

He looked down. Maynard had freed himself from the phone cord. Then he dragged his limp body to the water cooler. He steadied himself with one hand as he downed a cup of water with the other. Just then a Cormorant flew by. Horrified, Maynard's knees buckled, the water splashed to the ground, and he collapsed onto the floor.

Quickly he struggled back to his feet. He opened his mouth, but no words came out. He dragged his body to the whiteboard near his desk. He picked up a green marker and with his left hand shaking he scribbled out a single word. It read,

"WORKSTATION."

He dropped the marker and steadied himself again. This time against his desk. Then, with his left hand still shaking, he pointed toward his workstation.

A message was flashing on his screen. It read,

"ALRC disabled. Do you want to re-enable Component?"

Lindsey instantly darted across the room. Without hesitation she picked up the snake, pointed, and clicked. Then she turned. A sound was coming from the far side of the room. It sounded like it was coming from just outside an open window. She moved toward it. The sound grew louder. She hesitated, then shook her head and leaned out the window.

Perched along the ledge, just a few feet from her, she saw two brightly colored birds.

"Lindsey!"

Hearing her name startled her.

"Lindsey! I need your help!"

She looked beyond the birds where the voice was coming from and saw her brother. He was grasping the side of the building with one hand and holding onto Aerial's lifeless body with the other. Without thinking she jumped out onto the six inch ledge. She was seven stories above the ground, and we already know how much she hates heights. But she didn't let that stop her, as she helped her brother drag Aerial off the ledge to safety.

Lindsey looked at her brother. He was still shaking.

"Pat, you could have froze, but you didn't. You didn't let your fear get in the way of doing what you knew you needed to do."

Chapter Twenty-Nine – A baseball cap

On the floor, motionless, lay Aerial's body.

"Good, he's still breathing."

"You should have seen us coming down!"

Pat was still excited about what he had done.

"I did see you. You caused quite a stir." She looked around as she said it.

"They'll be searching for us soon. They know we're here now." A look of concern crossed her face.

"Aerial made me practice for hours and hours." She reached over and pulled open a closet door.

"Quick, in here."

She held the door open as Pat and Mike carried Aerial's unconscious body into the closet. They laid him on the floor. Pat looked up at his sister.

"I had trouble at first." She was looking at Aerial.

"I got blisters on my hands."

The boy stuck his palms in front of his sister's face. She wasn't paying attention to him now. Aerial still wasn't moving and she didn't know at this point if he was alive or dead.

"See."

He pushed his hands right up almost touching her nose. Lindsey looked at her brother thinking that the boy still doesn't know when to shut up. She was still thinking about how serious the situation was, and her brother was just jabbering away like he always did. She stopped and looked at him.

"Pat, you need to start thinking about college and your future."

"Why? I'm not so sure college is right for me."

"But Pat you have to go to college. The world is changing. You have to get a college degree so you can have a successful life."

"And you think I need college to be successful? If I went to college I'd probably end up majoring in some useless subject like Sociology and then I wouldn't find a decent job for years!"

Lindsey just shook her head.

"We'll discuss this later. There are more important matters we need to attend to right now."

Then she cracked open the closet door so she could see Maynard. He had a screwdriver in his hand, and was opening up the back of his workstation. She wondered, what on earth was he doing?

He removed a metal plate and reached inside. He squinted. Then he stretched his arm further into the computer and grunted. He was focused on reaching something that seemed to be tightly wedged between the disk and memory. He was poking at it with the screwdriver.

Then he removed his arm from the back of his machine and placed the screwdriver down. He reached back in with his bare hand giving, whatever it was, one good yank. Then he tumbled to the floor.

Quickly he stood back up. He was dazed and his eyes began to roll. But when he shook his head the rolling instantly stopped.

"There, I got it!"

He carefully examined the heavy wrinkled cloth he held in his right hand. It was red and blue. Slowly he unraveled it.

"It's a cap," he muttered to himself. "A baseball cap. How did a baseball cap get inside my computer?"

He turned and scratched his head with his left hand as he smiled. Then he placed the Atlanta Braves baseball cap firmly on his head. But as he did his eyes began to roll again. Then his legs gave way and he collapsed onto the floor trembling. A moment later the trembling stopped.

Aerial was now waking up and starting to move. He was looking at Maynard as he lay motionless on the floor.

"I think he needs medical attention," Aerial calmly stated. He looked at Mike as he pointed to a medical emergency kit hanging on the wall.

"Grab that stretcher. We need to get him out of here."

Chapter Thirty – Was it a test?

"I haven't been completely honest with you."

Lindsey looked up at Aerial as they walked behind Pat and Mike who were carrying Maynard on the stretcher down the hall toward the exit from the Jefferson Lab.

"When you knocked on my door I knew it was you. I've known your father a long time."

"What was it about?"

"It was about the kids."

"Was it a test?"

"No. Your father never cared for tests. He believed tests just lead to answering questions the way someone else sees the world. He didn't believe in measuring students on facts they just memorized. He was more interested in teaching them how to solve real world problems using their own brain power."

Aerial hesitated.

"Your father had a plan. But it didn't go like he planned it."

He shook his head.

"It was supposed to be about learning from your mistakes."

Aerial chuckled.

"I guess he didn't count on making a few of his own."

"The demonstration of his hybrid virtual reality-reality engine must have slipped his mind. God knows he never would have planned it on that day. He's not that crazy. When you fell through the window it should have been stopped right then. The window was only intended for us to monitor your learning experience. But Aerial figured out how to use it as an escape route."

He turned and looked at the girl.

"Your father wanted it to be real, but not that real. None of you were ever supposed to end up in the Jefferson Lab. You don't know how close we came to losing you and Mike."

The color drained from the girl's face and her voice was shaking as she replied to Aerial.

"How did you meet my father?"

"He was my mentor. He taught me things others said I couldn't learn. But I did learn and faster than any of them thought I could. And it scared them. They told Fred to shut me down. They told him I could hurt people. But they didn't know what else I could do. Your father did, and he was willing to take the risk."

Aerial hesitated. They were approaching the exit from the Jefferson Lab.

"When they sent your father away they said it was because of what he did to your DNA using CRISPR, but that was a smokescreen. They really wanted to put an end to his groundbreaking research related to kids learning what they really need to know to survive in life. When the universities got wind of what he was doing they lobbied Washington to cut off the funds to his research, and then I think you know the rest of the story."

The man who had shown Lindsey and Mike around the Lab was headed toward the exit with a young boy he had interviewed. Lindsey recognized the boy. He was the tall lanky boy with stringy blond hair she talked to near Snake River.

"Hello Lindsey. This is Al. We interviewed Al a few months ago, but we didn't hire him because senior management didn't think he'd fit in with the way we do things here at the Lab. But for some unknown reason the thinking of our leadership has suddenly changed and they want to give him a second look."

The man, and Al continued moving down the hall toward the exit.

Aerial looked at the girl.

"Your father may have made some mistakes. But what you just saw is proof that his hybrid virtual reality-reality engine really works. It's also proof that you kids succeeded on your mission. I suspect how things are done here at the Lab are changing."

The girl looked at Aerial.

"But why did he keep it all a secret?"

"He wasn't allowed to talk, and frankly your father thought by the time he got out of prison you kids wouldn't even remember him."

The girl reached up putting her hand over her mouth and began shaking her head.

"Look Lindsey, I understand how you feel about your father trying to make you into someone different from who you are. But don't forget he never touched your brother's DNA and he's still trying to figure out who he is too!

Conclusion

It was one of those frigid winter days in Farthington. The McMichael's and North's sat five rows back of the home team's bench. They had sat in those same seats for every home game over the past two seasons. It was the last time they would sit in those seats together.

At the intermission Farthington trailed by four points. Janet and Fred were chatting with old friends from the Jefferson Lab.

"How are things out at the lab Jack?"

"Things were fine until last week."

"Did you hear about Maynard?"

"Hear what?"

"We lost him."

"Oh no! Was it his heart?"

"No, nothing like that."

"He resigned. He's giving the senior baseball league a shot. He signed with the Braves outfit."

A few feet away Mike and Pat were chatting.

"How's your father's project going out at the lab?"

"My father doesn't work there anymore. He's got some new big idea he's working on now all alone. He and my mother bought a place near the ocean. He told mom to pick it out. She's going to start her own business. He said he doesn't care what the place looks like as long as the garage is twice as big as the one on Cherry Street."

"What's your father's new idea?"

"I'm not sure, but its got something to do with Lindsey and Erin. He says he doesn't think it was just a coincidence how they ran into each other, and he thinks we all have clones out there. I think he's looking for another gate."

Later that evening the North family was planning to fly west to start their new life.

After the game the boys decided to spend their final few hours together with a walk through the Chestnut Hill Mall. They passed McFealy's pet store. A kitten in the window reminded Pat of Rosie and the old tunnel.

"Let's promise to get together."

"Ok. We'll make it a tradition," replied Pat. "I like traditions."

"Where should we meet next year?" Pat rubbed his chin.

"It really doesn't matter, Mike, as long as it isn't a quiet little town."

Epilogue

Maynard Jackson went on to throw four no hitters in the senior league and won 104 games and was unanimously elected to the senior baseball league hall of fame. He continued to pitch in the senior league until he was 94 years old. And yes, in case you were wondering, Maynard was one of the three missing ALRCs.

Mike North moved to Colorado in the winter of 2023. In the 2028 Winter Olympics Mike was first alternate on the United States downhill Ski Team. He then returned to Farthington to teach junior Olympian hopefuls at the same ski school where he learned from his father.

Fred E. McMichaels received a suspended sentence when he agreed to plead guilty to illegal cloning of his daughter. He retired and moved to a new home near the ocean where he took up science fiction writing.

Janet McMichaels remains the calm and steady rock of the McMichael's family. She started her own business, a specialty dress shop, near their ocean retirement home. In her spare time she continues to enjoy all kinds of science fiction books with the one exception being anything written by her dear husband Fred.

Meg Savich and her husband Bill, along with JR Trip and his wife Sue, have become life-long friends of Janet and Fred and spend every New Year's Eve together.

Lenny continued working at the Jefferson Lab moving his way up the corporate ladder. As of the publication of this book, he had become the youngest person ever to hold the position of President of the company.

Patrick McMichael's went to college following the advice of his sister Lindsey and, as he predicted, majored in Sociology and thereafter struggled to find meaningful work for about ten years. However, he then became an entrepreneur and was named in 2030 to Forbes list of the ten richest men in America.

Erin, the full clone daughter of Fred and Janet became the music director at a high school about 20 miles west of Farthington. She received international acclaim for her innovative way of teaching music where you can practice without holding your instrument in your hand.

Jay Wilson, who the neighborhood kids all thought was crazy and lived with rats, was befriended by Fred when he found out that his son had hit him in the head with a rock he pegged right through Jay's front window. Fred gave Jay a little help and in return Jay agreed to help Fred on his secret project by playing the role of Aerial. Jay Wilson, alias Aerial, was, in fact, the second missing ALRC.

Lindsey McMichaels, the daughter of Fred and Janet, who Fred had gone to jail for five years for illegally using the CRISPR technology to increase her height to aid her basketball career, was drafted by the women's professional basketball association, but failed to make the team. She then moved to Canada to play professional basketball in the Canadian woman's professional league. Due to the new immigration laws in the United States she has not been able to get back into the country, but Fred's sister, Ann, and brother-in-law, Dick, who live near the Canadian border, just outside Buffalo, have been keeping an eye on her.

The third missing ALRC was Al, the tall lanky boy with stringy blond hair.

About the Author

 Fred E. McMichaels is the pen name of Paul E. McMahon. I use a pen name primarily to keep my fiction writing separate from my technical business writing. I am an independent software engineering coach, consultant and author. When I am not coaching software teams I enjoy long distance running, golf and writing science fiction stories that conceivably could happen in the not too distant future.

Note from the author

If you would be so kind, please consider writing a review of the book on Amazon.com. This is one of the few ways that self-published authors like myself can compete with the big name authors and publishing companies. If you do write a review of the book, please email me at pemcmahon@acm.org so I can send you an interesting story about a possible alternative ending to the book I considered, and I will explain why I decided not to use it. This is my small way of saying, Thank You.